Sunrise

Inspired by True Events

Theresa Valentine

ISBN: 150093268X
ISBN 13: 9781500932688
Library of Congress Control Number: 2014915275
CreateSpace Independent Publishing Platform
North Charleston, South Carolina

We can't help everyone,
But everyone can help someone.

Chapter 1

The Show

As I drove into the New York City news center to meet one of the country's most admired talk show hosts for a featured story about a woman who struggled and survived a difficult and threatening relationship, I reflected on the years and the challenges I had faced. I wondered how many women endured similar circumstances as I and would learn a little about their own internal fortitude and personal courage in the one-hour show. Would they connect with me, or would they judge me?

I parked my car in the spot marked "show guest" and then slowly turned off the engine, rolled up the windows, and stepped outside. I closed my eyes and raised my face to the sky to breathe in the clean air as the morning rays warmed my face. I couldn't help but just smile. I'm sure people walking by must've thought I was weird with my face to the sky and a grin from ear to ear, but I didn't care. The thought crossing my mind at that second was just how lucky I was. It had been such a trip. Here I was; it had taken years, but I was ready to share my experiences with others. I was blessed.

Within seconds my mind took a turn for the practical. My next thoughts were, *God, I hope I don't bawl my way through the show! I can hear my girls now: "Mom, you're such a baby!"* As I laughed, inside my head,

I thought, *Some things will never change. I will never change… Well, maybe that's not totally true. In many ways, I have changed.*

I entered the tall gray building with the large television call numbers across the top and walked slowly to the security guard. The foyer must have been ten stories high with grey and white marble floors and gray marble walls. I introduced myself and explained that I was there for that day's show. He directed me to the reception area, asked if I would like a drink, and invited me to sit and relax in the green room. Beside me was an amazing spread of assorted snacks, drinks, and books to pass the time. I settled in with the latest fashion magazine, a Diet Coke, and a little grin.

It was about thirty minutes before Sarah Swanson, the number-one talk show host in America, popped her head into the green room to see how I was doing.

"Five minutes to show time. Are you ready?"

That's a funny question, I thought. *Is anyone ever really ready to share their most private experiences with the world?* I turned and smiled. "I'm as ready as I'll ever be."

Sarah explained that a technician would be by to pick me up when she was ready to introduce me.

"After I open the show and complete my morning monologue on current events, I'll bring you on stage. You should just relax. You have an inspiring story to share, and I believe similar stories are secretly played out behind closed doors in many homes across the country. Let's just enjoy ourselves today. It'll be a great show."

I smiled though I could feel the sweat start to expand from my neckline clear down the center of my back. As beads began to form and roll south, my first thought was that I knew I had selected the right outfit. After years of public speaking and sweaty nervousness, I was confident there wouldn't be sweat stains showing under my arms. Black—the best color for nervous presenters. My black suit was my power suit. Plus, shouldn't the black slim off the fifteen pounds the camera would put on?

I took one more look at myself in the mirror as the makeup artist put the last touch of powder on my face and thought, *Damn, you're not so bad for a forty-something-year-old woman. All right, so there are some wrinkles around the eyes and some age spots here and there—and oh yeah, those "parentheses" around my mouth, but those are my smile lines. Something to be proud of! Those marks tell the world that I've laughed out loud quite a bit to create those beautiful lines. I'm glad I picked the dark-green lace camisole for under my suit—just enough neckline showing, skirt is not too short, gray twill heels with the little black bow are not too high. Sophisticated, sexy—I can do that.* I put on the brown rectangular glasses for that little extra self-confidence. *Whew! I think I'm ready to go.*

With the knock on the door, I stood up, brushed off the wrinkles from my skirt and jacket, tucked my bra strap tightly under my shoulder pad, and followed the production assistant out of the room and down the hall to the backstage entrance.

As I stood in the wings, waiting for Sarah to complete my introduction, I had that surreal feeling. This was the second time in my life I had had that out-of-body, am-I-sure-this-is-my-life feeling. This one, I felt, would have a much more positive ending than the last time. I listened from the wing as Sarah went live. "Today, we have a very special guest star. She could be any one of us, and I believe you'll see she is many of us: a mom and a corporate business woman, balancing home and work expectations, dealing with a difficult divorce, and finding humor and self-confidence along the way. She made the choice to leave a marriage and venture into a new world where she knew there would be challenges. Through it all, she has been an inspiration to other women who have feared the unknown. She has demonstrated courage and resiliency, and most of all, she has taught her daughters and many women whose lives she's touched how to become strong and independent and to be able to deal with whatever life throws their way. She says she wouldn't change a thing. Let's listen to her story, and at the end of our show, ask yourself if you were in her shoes, as I ask her again, what would you change? Please join your hands as we welcome Stephanie Towers to our show."

Slowly, I crossed the twenty feet of the stage from the wing to the brown leather chairs positioned squarely in the center. As I approached Sarah, I reached out my hand and said, "Thank you for that spirited introduction; I'm very happy to be here."

Sarah began by saying, "When I first heard about your volunteerism to assist women and young adults who are not in healthy relationships or who are facing tough decisions, I was in awe that you would actually spend your free time in this capacity. You may not have known, but I watched one of your presentations at the local community college and was so moved by your story and the reaction of the women in the audience that I wanted you to come and share your story with my national audience. When we posted the topic of this show on our website, the seats filled in less than two hours. There was a waiting list of attendees for the show. That says a lot about what goes on behind closed doors in America and how so many women want to learn how to make a difference in their own lives."

"I'm glad you had the opportunity to attend one of my presentations. When I received your director's call, I was wondering how you found me. Over the past six months, as I began sharing my story, I found that about 90 percent of attendees at my presentations are women. I think the men who do attend are coerced by their spouses or significant others but find that they walk away learning a little something about the women in their lives."

"That's a good thing," said Sarah.

"What started as a part-time ambition to help others has become my full-time mission. For the first time in my life, I feel like I am truly making a difference, leaving footprints on this world for those to see when I depart. Some would argue that working full-time and helping a company become prosperous would be making a difference. But I always felt there was more I could do. It wasn't the fulfilling life I'd dreamed of. Now, I'm helping people see life in a different way, maybe make different choices in their own lives. This is why I went through everything I did. I know that now. This is where I'm supposed to be. Sarah, let me ask you, when you look at me, what do you see?"

"I see an energetic, beautiful, confident woman."

"After you heard my story, did you see the same?"

"I saw you the same with a lot of respect for what you've been through. Have you thought about the impact of telling your story?"

"I thought about it for years before I decided to share. I know there are many reasons why I wouldn't share my experiences—the potential to hurt those that I love when they hear about how I viewed their interactions in my life, my children's and parents' reactions to what experiences I've gone through, extended family and friends who may be embarrassed by me, and the potential impact to my career based on the reactions of the coworkers, peers, managers, and executives at work. But with that said, I believe there are more positive reasons to share than negative reasons not to. I think I've been through something that women can relate to. For those of you who know me best, you'll understand this. On the pros and cons list, the pros won."

"With all those potential negatives, why take the risk?"

"Isn't life about taking risks, leaping forward into the unknown on a wing and a prayer? If I can make a difference to one person in this world who feels that she is all alone and trapped in a relationship where she cannot break out, that she has no choices, no options, no hope, then I did the right thing by coming here today to share my story. Hopefully, she can learn something about herself through my choices, my struggles, my happiness, my losses, and my loves. Perhaps she will find the same strength I found in family, friends, and most importantly, in myself, and she can take the steps to move in the right direction as I did. For every teenage girl who thinks that a boy in her life will make her happy or complete, I hope she can see that she can make herself happy…and until we are happy alone, we will never be happy with others."

"Any other reasons?"

"Yes, two very special reasons. My daughters. I hope from my experiences they learn that life is not always smooth, but that every step along the way, they have choices. They own their choices. They are in control. I love my girls with all my heart. They are my greatest pride and my greatest joy. If I had never gone down the paths of life laid out before me, they would not be here with me. I believe there are no right or wrong choices in life. Paths we choose lead us to new paths. All the paths lead to our future. Our future is what we make of it. It's just hard to see how the path cuts through the trees and where it will take you. That's where the leap of faith comes in."

"Are your girls here?"

"No. I actually did not tell my family I was coming because I wanted to do this on my own."

"What would you say to them if they were here?"

"I would tell them the same thing I tell them every day. You have a choice as to how you face the day every morning. You choose whether to be happy or miserable. Choose to be happy, to see the bright side of any gloomy situation—it's there, but sometimes you just have to look hard to find it. Believe it or not, every choice I made was made based on the love for you girls. Was I a perfect mom? No, I've made mistakes along the way, but that's life. When we don't have an instruction book, we have to make decisions as we see best at the time. Although it hasn't always been easy raising two strong, independent women, I wouldn't change one moment of it. I love you both with all of my heart and soul. I am very proud of who you've become and who you are yet to become."

"I can't wait for our viewers to hear your story. Start us off this morning with the most important thing you've learned."

"Hmm…There's so much. If I had to sum it into one statement, it would be: 'What you experience is not who you are. How you react is who you become.'"

"Wow, that's really a profound statement. Do you always think like that?"

"Throughout the challenging periods in my life, I always thought you can let life take you where it does or you can direct your own destiny. You'll hear this a lot from me today - *choice*. It's a gift we all have but don't frequently use. We are all actors and actresses, showing only what we want to the world to see. There is no perfect life, no 'American dream.' Life is a journey, not a destination to reach. Every day brings adventures with highs and lows that teach you something about yourself. Embrace each event with energy and enthusiasm.

"As you'll hear, there have been many events in my life that brought me to my knees, to the darkest points of my life, but in each, I searched deep down and found the strength to see the positive and make the best of what I was dealt. I didn't let life lead me. I created my life. I decided to be right here, right now."

Chapter 2

The Early Years

"Tell us a little about your life. Start at the beginning with your family. I understand that your childhood was pretty normal and you got married really young?"

"Yes, pretty normal. Yes, very young. There were five us in our family: my parents, my older sister (ten months my senior), and my brother (four years my junior). We lived in a five-room home with three bedrooms and one bath. It was a small green ranch with yellow shutters and a yellow front door. As a matter of fact, that was the first house my parents purchased when they were married over forty-five years ago, and they still reside there today. The town was a lazy, quiet, nothing-to-do town. As I was growing up, I knew we didn't have a lot of money, but I knew my parents loved us all very much. Our cars were old, and my dad did all the maintenance himself from oil changes to tying tin cans onto the exhaust pipe to stifle the loud muffler sound and placing wood on the rotten floorboards so you didn't see right through to the road below. My sister and I were mortified growing up with what seemed like the oldest and noisiest cars in town. We were embarrassed at times and would duck down in the backseat when we drove by people we knew. It was only when we got older that we appreciated that an old/noisy car was better than no transportation at all. Dad was an electrician by trade and worked very hard to keep food on our table and clothes on our backs. My mom was a homemaker.

She volunteered at school, shuttled us around as we got older, and attended every sporting event we had. She was home for us every day when we got off the bus from school, and every night, dinner was on the table where we ate as a family—five o'clock sharp, simple traditions frequently lost in today's fast-paced world with crazy schedules and busy families.

"Every day after school, we'd go out and play with the neighborhood kids. There were a bunch of kids our age, and we'd stay out until we heard our mothers standing at the front door screaming our names. We knew it was dinnertime, and we knew we had to scurry home quick. After dinner, it was dishwashing or drying time. I hated both jobs. My sister and I would rotate the washing and drying; my brother, baby brother, didn't have to do anything, or so it seemed that way to my sister and me.

"During the summers we would spend a week on vacation at the state park camping. I didn't realize until I was older that was the only vacation my parents could afford. Finances were tight, and there were times when the money my dad made just barely paid the bills. They were religious people, so, by default, we kids were religious people. Every Saturday afternoon, we would sit in the front pew of St. Matthew's Church as a family and attend four o'clock Mass. As kids, we hated it. Many years later, when I had my own children, I understood the importance of faith and family rituals."

Sarah asked, "Going to church wasn't such a bad thing?"

I thought for a second and replied, "No, it was a good thing. I just didn't appreciate it until many years later.

"At school, we had to use lunch food coupons; that was pretty embarrassing as a kid. But there wasn't a choice, so my sister and I stood proud and tall and marched through the food line to hand in the free lunch voucher. Every once in a while, some kid would make fun of us, as kids would do, but it didn't happen too much. We'd just grin and walk away.

"I was a chubby kid between fifth and sixth grade, which resulted in the nickname of 'cow' in school. It was tough being picked on—every time you came up to kickball, having your classmates 'moo' and being the last one picked for a team. Tough on a kid's self-esteem. Many days, I came home in tears, and on a few occasions in the sixth grade, I was beaten up by a mean girl named Tracy. Years later, when I had my own girls, it was those types of memories that helped in the decision to send them to Catholic school from pre-K to eighth grade for Courtney and pre-K to twelfth grade for Chloe. Those tough kid lessons reminded me to treat others as you would like to be treated—no matter what the circumstances. It's funny how those memories remain with me after all these years. In junior high school I was more of an introvert and a little more 'street wise.' I focused on my schooling.

"It was in seventh grade that I had my first boyfriend and met a young man who would end up being one of my best friends through high school. I started to slim down and began to attend dances. I joined basketball and cheerleading and in the eighth grade became the captain for both teams. I was honored with MVP trophies and awards and was pretty confident as I entered high school. At five-seven, I weighed around a hundred and twenty pounds and had long blond hair and a tan to die for. I ended up graduating top of my junior high school class, beating the 'smart boy' by just points.

"Home life was still good during these years. My sister and I got along pretty well, minus her occasional hair pulling and our nail-scratching catfights. Those are the fights that only sisters could have. Granted, she did torture me with the plastic snakes under my bed and under my pillows, but she directed most of her 'bugging' to my brother. Being the middle child, I tried to keep everyone happy. I felt it was my job to keep everything balanced. As my brother got older, he was into his sports and my dad was involved with coaching his activities like

Little League. I rarely got into trouble during those years. My brother and sister got into enough trouble for all of us.

"It was around the beginning of high school that I noticed my dad occasionally drank. I remember one Christmas Eve when he was not home by 3:45 p.m., his typical time to arrive, my mom was very nervous and upset. When she began to pace, I knew something was wrong. Eventually, my dad showed up, and we kids were ushered into our rooms where we were advised to stay as Mom dealt with Dad. He was clearly drunk. That was a night that would stick in my mind forever. As he lay on the living room floor totally wasted, he rolled over, fell on the manger, and broke the heads off a few of the ceramic pieces that Mom had so beautifully crafted in class. I think Jesus was saved, but Joseph was beheaded.

"Soon after that incident, it became apparent that Dad did have a drinking problem, and when Mom went away on vacation, my sister and I would get the wrath of his disposition—lectures about life, mostly. He was never mean. He wasn't a nasty drunk. He was a lecturer on life. The last thing a teenager wants—life lectures. It sucked. It was shortly after high school that Dad stopped drinking, and no future family event would ever offer alcohol. Just became something we really never talked about, but we just adjusted with the 'no drinking' party rule."

Sarah asked, "Tell us about high school. How would you describe those four years?"

"I went from a small Catholic junior high school to the large public high school. The sheer size of the school was overwhelming, never mind trying to remember my class schedule and locker combination. I had my locker combination written in every book I owned for fear I would forget it and be without one of my books for class. It was the very first day of school when I met my very best friend. We were like Mutt and Jeff—total opposites who connected immediately. At five-seven with blond hair and green eyes, I was a stark contrast to my new friend, who was no more than five feet with dark-brown hair and dark-brown eyes. She was the extroverted, crazy cheerleader, and I was the introvert. Yes, I am an introvert—believe it or not! Many thought I was a bitch throughout my high school and college years, but I was just shy (and misunderstood!).

"If you asked my sister about me in high school, she'd describe me in three words: *Goody Two Shoes.* Yes, she would be correct. I didn't smoke pot or cigarettes (and still haven't) and didn't drink alcohol. I was on the honor roll most of the years and graduated in the National Honor Society.

"I played flute in the band for four years and was the drum major for the band in my senior year. I tried basketball my freshman year but twisted my ankle severely and then decided not to pursue the sport. Instead, I got a job at a local Catholic church rectory and worked there from the time I was fifteen until I accepted my first full-time job. I made dinner for the priests and worked in the office.

"When I turned sixteen, I began dating. I had some different boyfriends and went to a junior prom when I was a sophomore, and then I met Mike, whom I dated for the last two years of school. I learned a lot about relationships in those two years."

"But you were not with him, correct?" Sarah asked.

"Correct. He broke up with me during the summer after we graduated, and I was devastated. *Dev-as-ta-ted.* I felt like life would not go on. He was my first love, and my heart was ripped out and stomped on. Did I mention I was devastated? It was every teenage girl's worst nightmare. I thought for sure he and I would be together forever, and I couldn't understand why he would walk away. When he asked me to wait until he was thirty and then we could get married, I laughed. Was he kidding? No way! Thirty was a million years from eighteen. I cried for weeks when he dumped me. My mom was very concerned, and I got very thin. I didn't eat, and I cried all the time. Looking back, I realize I was probably borderline anorexic. Once I dealt with the fact that life would go on, I realized the drama wasn't worth it. To this day, I will not have a scale in my house. It's too easy to get obsessed. Teenage boys are such an obsession for teenage girls, and teenage girls get so wrapped up in their looks, material items, and relationship drama.

"My senior year was amazing. I enjoyed school, participated in the Miss Teen Connecticut pageant, and was part of the homecoming court. It was a year full of fun, friends, shopping, and guys. It was everything I had hoped high school would be. I was the ideal high school girl for my parents and gave them nothing to worry about.

"I graduated in June 1985 and decided to go to the community college for secretarial sciences. I spent one year there full-time when I was recruited to join the local insurance company through their secretarial intern program. Through that program, I met the most phenomenal boss who would end up being a great career mentor throughout the years—Tony. I was in awe of how he could get his teams to follow him into any battle and never got flustered when the pressure was on. He taught me how to manage the most difficult situations and handle myself professionally in a corporate environment. I owe him a lot of credit for believing in me, leading by example, and helping me grow into the leader I am today. Unfortunately, he recently passed away. There are many people he touched in his life, one of which was me. He will never be forgotten."

Sarah interjected, "So, things are going well. Life is moving along. You have a job, and you're finishing your schooling. How about the love life? Anything there?"

I thought for a moment and said, "No, not really, dating here and there and hanging out with my girlfriends. Pretty typical post-high-school stuff. Then, the year after high school, I met the girls' father."

"Stephanie, tell us how you met."

And so I began, "It was 1986, the year of stretch stirrup pants and big hair. The more hairspray we piled on the better. Boy, did I have the hair! I look back now and think, *If only I had stock in Aqua Net.* It was super-extra hold that got the job done.

"My girlfriend Mel and I decided to volunteer coaching our former junior high school girls' basketball team of seventh- and eighth-graders.

"It was the first game of our season, and we were all sitting on the bench at Immanuel Lutheran School waiting for the referee to arrive. It's interesting how I can even remember the school as if it was yesterday—brick building that you park in the back, walk down the hallway past the trophy cabinet, and the gym was on the left. The ref was late, and Mel and I were nervous wrecks since it was our first game. I had my bright-pink stretch pants on—looking hot (or so I thought at the time, looking back, not so much). Finally, five minutes after the game was supposed to start, I heard someone announce that the ref had arrived. I looked up to see a tall, dark, handsome young man walk across the basketball court. Our eyes met instantly. I turned to Mel, and we both giggled (as girls do at twenty) about how hot he was! Wow!"

"That was Kevin?" Sarah asked.

"Yes, my future husband. I was mesmerized. I felt my 'Prince Charming' just walked into my life through the entrance door of a basketball court and into my heart. It was amazing—just like the fairy tales we read as children. When the doors flew open it was like there were fireworks and fairy dust flying all around him. Okay, maybe that's more like what we'd see in a cartoon, but you get the idea. It was magical.

"It wasn't until after the fourth game that he actually had more of a conversation with me other than just a hello. He restructured his schedule to be the referee at all of our remaining games. I thought that was super cool. We didn't have a winning season that year. Our team was pretty bad; however, there were probably more calls in our favor than there would have been with another referee.

"The last game of the season arrived, and finally, he mustered the courage to see if we wanted to go out after the game. Mel and I went to the local bar/restaurant and had a bite to eat and drink. Of course I, being Miss Goody-Two-Shoes would not normally do such a thing, but he was so handsome and charismatic that against my good judgment, I went. A few drinks later and a good night kiss at my car and I was hooked. From that moment on, we spent almost all of our free time together.

"We had dated for about a year when he asked me to marry him. The proposal wasn't particularly romantic, more matter-of-fact."

With a sly glance, Sarah grinned and asked, "How'd he ask you?"

"We were at my house, and he was sitting on the couch when I came over and sat on the armrest. He then pulled the ring box out of his jacket with shaking hands, told me he loved me, and asked if I would marry him. Apparently, my mom knew about the plan and had helped to pick out the ring. It was a quarter carat diamond—and size didn't matter at that time. I knew he loved me, and I was in love with him. I said yes."

"No romance, no dropping to one knee, roses, or champagne or music and dancing?"

"Nope. It really didn't matter back then, but it's interesting when you look back on your life how it was a prelude to what was to come. We were so immature, so needing each other to move on with our lives in different ways. So young and in love."

"And stupid?"

"Not sure I'd say 'stupid' but more immature and unprepared for marriage."

"What do your girls think about getting married so young?"

"I tell them all the time, 'Don't get married young. When you're young, you still have so much growing to do. People change so much between ages twenty and thirty. Even if you meet the man of your dreams, have a very long engagement.'

"Anyway, I digress. Sarah, aren't you supposed to keep me on target?"

Sarah laughed with a little smirk and clearly put me back on track. "Let's get to the wedding and the wedding night." She winked.

"So the next year was wedding planning. For anyone, at any age, wedding planning is so exciting and at the same time, very stressful. But we got through the plans and the showers and everything we needed to do, and before we knew it, the wedding day had arrived."

Chapter 3

Should I, or Shouldn't I?

"In November 1987, we were married. It was a beautiful fall evening. The whole bridal party had spent the afternoon together getting our hair and makeup professionally done. I was a beautiful bride. It was so picture perfect."

Sarah asked, "Before we get to the wedding details, tell me—was there ever a time where you thought this is the wrong decision, that you shouldn't get married?"

"It's amazing how clear everything is after the fact—What's the saying?—Hindsight is 20/20? Yes, there were things that I saw retrospectively. There is one primary incident that we had where I think my whole family wondered if I was doing the right thing."

"What happened?"

"One afternoon, we were at my house just hanging out. It was a few weeks before the wedding, and we were sitting on the side hill of the yard. For no apparent reason, Kevin just started to get angry. He started to yell about how I hated his friends and because of me, he wasn't able to go out and hang with the guys as much as he wanted to. From my perspective, this was not true. I had never stopped him. He demanded my engagement ring be returned to him as he screamed at me. I tried to reason, to beg, and to plead that we could work it out, that we could talk it out. No reasoning. So I reluctantly slipped that diamond off my finger and handed it over. He grabbed it and threw it down the hill to the neighbor's yard, stormed out of the backyard, jumped into his car, and took off. I was mortified, angry, and very embarrassed. I prayed that my parents hadn't overheard that crazy argument.

"I sat there for about an hour, composed myself, and then went into the house. Later that evening, Kevin called to apologize and begged for my forgiveness. I accepted his apology. I wondered years later as the outbursts continued over no special reason if there was a bigger issue here. I could never understand what I did to deserve that treatment. Never could. It was random and unprovoked. So to answer your question, it was at that moment I wondered if marrying him was the right choice."

"Did your parents say anything to you?"

"Later that evening, my dad came to me and asked if there was an issue. He had been in his garden in the afternoon. Of course, I lied and said everything was just fine. I couldn't admit it, but I had my doubts. Even with the doubts, I was not going to walk away. I was a fighter, not a quitter, and I wasn't going to leave. I'd made a commitment, and I was going to make it work—no matter what! There was a promise on my left hand—well, actually at this time, it was in the lawn somewhere, but you know what I'm saying. It was a promise."

"You must have had so many things running through your head: do you stay, delay the wedding, walk away and break off the relationship?"

"It was horrible. Part of me felt like I should just walk away and not worry about what everyone would think."

"But you couldn't walk away?"

"I couldn't, and I was so mad at myself for it. I had this overwhelming feeling that I would be disappointing everyone. I didn't want my family to be disappointed in me, and I decided it was more important that I not disappoint and to continue with the marriage plans."

"So you chose potential unhappiness over perceived disappointment?"

"Yes, I guess you could explain it that way. In retrospect, that is what I did. I can remember the talk I had with my mother a few days before my wedding. She said, 'If you don't love him, don't do it. If he doesn't treat you well, walk away. We can call it off, every last detail, no worries. No one will be upset, and no one will be angry.' It was then that I found out she had seen that whole display of asinine behavior and she was concerned that I was not making the right choice for me. Turns out, she was standing on her hope chest and perched cautiously staring through the folds of her curtains out her bedroom window as she watched the events unfold that afternoon on the side yard of our home."

"What happened to the ring?"

"The next morning, when I knew everyone was still asleep, I went outside and found it nestled in the blades of grass at the bottom of the hill by the row of pine trees. I slipped it back on my finger and we pretended like nothing had ever happened.

"I cried the night before my wedding and had this very heavy heart. I didn't know the difference between instinct to run and cold feet. At forty-seven, I know what the difference is. At twenty, I did not. I remember someone once said to me a few years ago, 'The wedding is just a party; the marriage is a commitment. Cancelling a wedding is just cancelling a party; it's not a big deal.'"

Quietly, Sarah asked, "So, you got married? You went through with it?"

"Yes, I did."

"Was it a beautiful wedding?"

"Yes, it was the first Friday of November, a beautiful fall evening. The air was crisp and cool with a slight northeast breeze gently blowing the leaves that were on the ground and whistling through the trees. I wore my mother's multilayered lace gown that made me look and feel like a princess. Since it was my mother's gown, there was a sentimental component, a connection between my mother and me. My sister was my maid of honor. Phil, Kevin's brother, was his best man. We had a small wedding party—two bridesmaids and two ushers with about seventy-five guests. Kevin looked very handsome that evening with his dark brown hair, brown eyes and a perfect body in a black tuxedo. Nothing better than a good looking guy in a tuxedo!

"As my father walked me down the aisle that evening, I can remember clear as day, that my wish—my secret wish—was that my friend Rob would come rushing through the doors of that church screaming, *Don't do it! He doesn't love you! I do!*"

"Who is Rob?"

With a smile, I began to explain. "Rob was the boy next door. He lived just a few streets away from my family's home. He had blonde hair, blue eyes and the gentlest soul. He was my best guy-friend throughout high school. We'd go places, like the annual hot air balloon festival, mini golfing or out for ice cream, just to hang out. We never quite connected as boy-friend/girl-friend; however there were many times over the years that one of us had feelings other than friendship for the other. The timing was just never quite right for us. Soon after I began dating Kevin, we lost touch. I haven't seen him in over 20 years, although through mutual friends, I know he did get married and has a few kids."

"So the door of the church didn't fly open?"

"Of course, you've figured; there was no knight in shining armor, no saving grace at the last moment. No fairy tale heroine rescued by a knight. I loved Kevin. Don't get me wrong. That was the problem. That was always the problem. Loved him and didn't want to walk away. But deep down in my heart, I didn't know if everything was going to work. *Would he change his behavior? Would he be the husband of my dreams and work with me to create the life that I dreamed of? Would the life that we talked about and dreamed about become reality?*

"There were tears streaming down my cheeks throughout the ceremony—tears of happiness that someone could love me as much as Kevin did and perhaps some tears of sorrow that there was a nugget of doubt in the back of my mind. After the ceremony ended, we took many family pictures before heading to our reception. We had a beautiful reception at a local restaurant.

"One shadow over the event was a bunch of Kevin's drunken friends (who were not invited to the wedding) decided to crash at the bar at the restaurant where we had the reception. It made for an uncomfortable time for me. Probably not an issue for him, but I thought, *What a bunch of immature idiots to do something like that!* I asked Kevin to ask them to leave, as they were making a scene, and he agreed. After he talked to them, they left quickly, and the rest of the evening went without a hitch. Between the first dance, the father's dance, the cake cutting, the garter toss, and throwing the bouquet, it was a picture-perfect wedding. It was what you dream of as a little girl, and I was the fairy princess bride.

"We took our honeymoon in the Bahamas. It was nice and romantic with hot days by the pool or the ocean or in town shopping. He drank; I drank—no problems. It was a nice time. It was more like a vacation than a romantic honeymoon. Maybe it was our age—still young and partying versus romantic and mushy? Maybe it was because I watched too many movies and had unrealistic expectations of what a honeymoon should be like. There wasn't romantic lovemaking as I had dreamed, but we did have a really nice time together. Soon, we were traveling back home and beginning our life together.

"Our life was good for the whole first year. We lived with my parents in the bedroom my sister and I had shared as kids for a few weeks after we were married while our new condo was being finished. We moved into our first home, our condo, for Christmas a few months after the wedding. It was very nice; it felt like playing house as a child. Our pattern was nice and comfortable. We woke together and spent time cooking dinner, watching TV, sleeping in each other's arms, and just enjoying each other's company.

"In less than a year, I got pregnant. All I could think was, *Oh, my, I'm gonna be a mom. Am I ready? I think I am, but is Kevin mature enough to be a dad?*"

"How'd you tell him? Anything romantic?"

"No, nothing romantic. After dinner one night, I approached him with the pregnancy stick that said 'plus.' *Surprise!*

"Kevin was excited once the shock wore off. My parents were excited. I was scared to death. I got fatter; he got drunker. *Drunker*, is that a word? Well, he began to drink more. Every weekend, he was out at the bar and I would sit home panicked, waiting for him to return. This ritual was all too familiar, as it brought me back to days of my childhood. I became my mother. I knew the exact time he should arrive home from work. One minute later and I felt the panic attack coming on. Not knowing how drunk he would be and what damage he would do when he would actually stroll into the house was a very difficult thing to deal with.

"Kevin wasn't a bad person; he just didn't know how to deal with bad things happening or stress in his life. The way he dealt with it was to drink. Listen to me; even now, I'm justifying his actions, and it's been over twenty-five years."

Sarah turned to the audience and asked, "Anyone in the audience know what that's like? Dealing with someone in your family who drinks to handle life?"

I thought inside my head, *Look how many heads are nodding "yes" in the audience. There are hands up all over the place.* There were too many women who had been in my shoes—way too many.

Sarah's words snapped me back to our conversation. "Tell me about what a typical night was like when Kevin was drinking."

"OK. Kevin arrived drunk home after work at least two times during the week and every Friday and Saturday night. I never knew what time he would arrive. But I did know that he would start a fight when he got home and something in the house would end up being broken. The next morning, he would be all apologetic, and I would be thinking of ways to cover up for whatever went wrong. We repeated this play again and again."

"Did you try to change the pattern once you saw the schedule?" Sarah inquired, half knowing the answer already.

"He didn't want to hear it. I don't think he cared what I thought. He was selfish in that way. He felt he had a rough day after work and it was okay to go out drinking to blow off some steam. Drinking was before me in his order of priority."

"So, the merry-go-round continued with no one getting off—week after week. Did things escalate over the year?"

"Yes. There was a night when I was seven months pregnant that I will always remember. All these years later, I can still give you every detail as if it happened yesterday. Close your eyes, and see this in your mind's eye. Imagine how you would feel.

"It was an early December Friday night, and Kevin wasn't home from work. I needed to go grocery shopping because I had a dinner party scheduled the next day. It was cold and lightly snowing when I left for the market at six. As I got home around eight, I drove into the condo parking lot to see that Kevin's truck was missing. He still wasn't home from work. Work ended at four and was twenty minutes away. I began to take the groceries out of the car. Did I mention I was as big as a house when I was pregnant? After a few bags were brought in, I had to begin to carry the heavy ones—you know, the ones filled with bottles of soda, cans, and jars. I was just a few steps away from the car, and the bag ripped open. The groceries flew out everywhere. Cans rolled under the car, and bottles of soda exploded. I began to crawl around the ground to gather up the groceries. All I could think was how much this grocery spill was a metaphor of my life—a mess. A big, fat, unbelievable mess. I sat down right in the middle of the parking lot, wrapped my arms around my big belly, grabbed my legs, and rocked back and forth crying gigantic tears. I could feel the anger and sadness building up. I was pregnant, and this was supposed to be the most wonderful time of our lives, but it wasn't. It was a sad time. I was alone, lonely, and scared. After a good twenty-minute sob, I composed myself, stood up, and gathered all the groceries from across the parking lot. I took multiple trips between the condo and the car to carry the rest of the groceries in. After putting them away, I sat quietly in the darkness of my living room and just breathed.

"I looked at the clock on the wall and noticed it was eleven and Kevin was still not home. I went upstairs to the bedrooms and began to pace back and forth—front bedroom to back bedroom, turning around and repeating the path. No lights on upstairs so no one could see me pace. I finally sat on a folding chair located in the front bedroom where I could look out the window of the baby's room to see all the cars entering the condo parking lot. I sat and watched for cars and cried. The next time I looked at the clock through a flood of tears pouring out of my eyes, it was one thirty, and there was still no Kevin.

"It was the first time that I felt I had had enough. This wasn't the life I chose. This wasn't the life I wanted. I was physically tired, and I was emotionally exhausted. What kind of relationship was I bringing my child into?"

"You had put up with this behavior for so long, what did you decide to do?"

"I grabbed a suitcase from the closet, shoved some of his clothes into it, got in the car, and started to drive away. I could feel my contractions starting due to the stress I was under, and I prayed to God that they would go away. Somehow through the tears, I drove across town to the bar, the bar he was always at. I knew I'd find him there with his drinking friends. I couldn't believe I was doing this. All I could think was, *I hope I don't make him angrier.* It was almost 2:00 a.m. *I had a party the next afternoon that I needed to get some rest for,* I thought as I parked the car. I was so beyond fed up that I didn't care. I was giving him his walking papers. I pulled up to his truck, looked around to ensure he wasn't watching, quietly pulled open the door, put the suitcase in the front driver's seat, and left a note taped to the suitcase that said, "Don't bother coming home."

"I shut the door, got back in my car, and drove back home. I knew there was a good chance that he would come home angrier than normal, but it was worth the risk. I needed to send him a message. It was 4:00 a.m., and I was still sitting in the front room upstairs staring out the window when I heard the truck pull up. I could feel the fear move from my toes to my nose. As the vomit rose into my throat, I said a short prayer that I hadn't made things worse for myself. At the same time all this fear was racing through my body, I felt a sense of anger that he was home and yet relief that he wasn't wrapped around a tree. I hated that I wished he was wrapped around a tree, and I hated that I wished he wasn't wrapped around a tree.

"I could hear him fumbling at the door trying to figure out how to get the key into the lock. In he came, stumbling into the foyer and banging around in the condo's kitchen. Next thing I heard was glass breaking and doors slamming.

"*Oh, shit,* I thought. *Now I have a freakin' mess to clean up.* There was a party in less than twelve hours.

"I took a deep breath and slowly and quietly tiptoed down the stairs to stop the mess. He began screaming and yelling, and I encouraged him to go up the stairs to bed. He screamed that this was his house and he would come and go when he pleased. He swore and screamed and screamed and swore. He was out of control. Nothing I said would calm him down. He was livid that I dared to tell him not to come home, that I left that suitcase in his car."

"Were you scared?" Sarah asked.

"Yes, I was afraid for me and my bulging baby belly. But I knew I needed to get him to settle down. If I didn't get things under control, the whole family would know about what was going on in our home. I couldn't have that. I knew I'd have to put on my happy face and pretend that everything was all right. I needed to go to sleep and to pull off the party. No one could know.

"*Be the actress,* I told myself. *Show the world what they want to see.* I knew I had to make things right—even if it meant I needed to take responsibility. So, I apologized for leaving the suitcase and told him that I was glad he was home. I knew that if I had sex with him, he would fall asleep and the evening would be over. No one (me) would get hurt. Loving him was the last thing I wanted to do. I felt no love for him—nothing. But I also knew that if I didn't, the evening would not end until he passed out. In my giant pregnant (not so sexy) body, I lured him upstairs. I couldn't kiss him. Every time he tried, I turned my head. I couldn't do it. To me, slow, passionate kissing is one of the most intimate aspects of lovemaking. I couldn't. His touch made me want to vomit as he did his thing. I just lay there. I felt as if I had been raped. I felt violated. A dirty whore doing a job, that was all it was. As he completed on top, I could feel the tears rolling down my face. After he rolled off, I could hear his breathing get slow and deep, and I knew he was asleep. I quietly rolled out of bed and headed downstairs and began to pick up the mess he had made.

"The vacuum cleaned up the shattered glass, and the glue repaired the cracked cabinet, but nothing in that house or in my life could repair my broken heart. I could feel my soul was crying as my eyes wept, and I soaked up the tears and blood off the floor. I had cut my finger on a piece of glass that had ripped through my skin. *Damn,* I thought, *this can't get worse.*

"I slept for two hours that night and in the morning, put the hemorrhoid paste under my eyes to reduce the swelling, put on my makeup, painted on my smile with a shade of burgundy lipstick, made platters of food, and baked until the house smelled warm and full of love. When the doorbell rang, I welcomed my guests into my home. Once again, no one knew. No one, that is, but me."

"God, why didn't you leave him? Kick his sorry butt out?"

"I asked myself that same question many times over the years. But I couldn't leave him; I felt too sorry for him, felt I could help him deal with his demons and create the life I wanted. Some days, I hated him, but more often, I still loved him. I was embarrassed because if I left, I would have failed. I couldn't. Not then. Not for a long time.

"During the last month of my pregnancy, I experienced two severe Braxton-Hicks sessions where I thought for sure I was in labor. Each resulted in visits to the emergency room and me being sent home hours later after the contractions stopped. Any pregnant woman knows that you want to be kept in the hospital, not sent home! The fact that I had to be returned home irritated Kevin since it required him to get out of work and bring me in and then bring me home and return to work. This was an inconvenience to him. This should have been a time of celebration as we awaited the birth of our child, but it wasn't. I didn't feel loved. I needed to feel loved. At least with the baby, I knew I would love that baby with all my heart, regardless of what happened with Kevin.

"At nine months pregnant, I was bigger than huge. During my early twenties, I didn't have a weight problem so I figured it wouldn't hurt to just eat what I wanted. I gained over seventy pounds, tipped the scale at two hundred, and was miserable. I had convinced my doctor to induce my labor on February 27 because I couldn't stand being so uncomfortable. It was scheduled for noon. Kevin was going to pick me up around 10:00 a.m., we would pick up Mom at the bowling alley from her Monday bowling league, and we would head to the hospital. When I woke that morning, I didn't feel well so I jumped in the shower and let the hot, pounding water from the shower beat on my beach ball stomach to reduce the cramping and lessen the pain.

"I stepped out of the shower, wiped myself down, took a step, and felt water pouring down my legs. After wiping a few more times, I realized my water had broken and ready or not, this baby was coming. I thought to myself - *this child was going to come on its time and not on mine.*

"This time, I didn't leave the hospital. After almost twelve hours of labor (only three of which were intense with the pushing), Courtney Ella Towers was born. Her independence on that day, being born on her schedule, was reflective of who she would become throughout her life. She had her own mind, her own opinion, her own schedule, and there was no changing that. That was so Courtney."

"How were things in your marriage after your daughter was born?"

"Unfortunately, not better. Kevin became less patient. Every time he would get angry, his method for dealing with it was to take off and get drunk. This typically meant speeding the truck out of the drive-way, heading to the bar to get drunk, come home angry, pick a fight, scream, and break something. It was the same pattern every time. The number of windows, doors, walls, cabinets, plates, cups, saucers, and glasses that were broken over the years can't be counted. I never knew if he would go to family functions, and I hesitated to commit because if he was drunk or angry, he would not go, and I would be left making excuses, so many excuses."

"No one in your family knew?"

"If they did, they didn't let on. God, I didn't want them to know. What would they think of me if they knew what I was dealing with? Would they believe me? Would they think I was making it up?"

"Do you think they would have judged you?"

"Back then, yes. Would they say I wasn't a good enough wife and that's why he behaved this way? That it was my fault? I couldn't risk that rejection. I kept silent.

"Now, I know differently. I know they would've been helpful. They would've supported me in my choices, given me strength. However, when you're in your early twenties, you don't always see things straight. That's why I'm sharing my story. I am hoping my lessons will help someone else see things clearer and sooner than I did. Much sooner."

"Did he ever physically hurt you?"

"There was one time that I'll tell you about it in a few minutes. There were more times when he hurt himself. There was one evening that was particularly bad. It was a Saturday afternoon, and Courtney was around one. He had come home after an afternoon at Spike's Bar - drunk, yelling and screaming as usual. He was in the garage throwing tools and screaming like a madman. I was in the house trying to determine what to do when he started banging at the door. I didn't let him in. I was scared. His anger was so intense that I thought this might be one of the times that he could hurt us. I locked the storm door to keep him out. After screaming at me to open it up, he put his arm through the glass door. There was blood everywhere. I mean *everywhere*—on the door, on the floor, on the steps. I don't deal with blood well. I faint, so this was even more difficult for me to physically handle on top of the emotions. I wanted him to bleed to death, but I knew I never would let that happen. He had clearly ripped open about six to eight inches of skin across his arm.

"As he stood there, he cried, begged for forgiveness, and asked me to care for him. I was so pissed at first, that I didn't know what I would do. However, after we went through two bath towels of blood, I drove him to the front door of the emergency treatment center as he sang his hymn of 'I'm sorry' and 'I'll stop,' and there I left him. He asked me to come back and get him later. I said, 'No, I don't think so. You figure out a way to get back to the house.'

"Courtney and I drove around for two hours that afternoon. Only by the grace of God were we kept safe as the tears poured down my face. I couldn't tell my family. I couldn't face the shame, the embarrassment. I needed them so much to hold me and tell me it would be OK, that they would help me leave this situation, that I didn't deserve this treatment, that it was OK to leave him. But I couldn't. So, I eventually drove home and faced my life.

"He walked home after twenty-two stitches were sewn into his arm. He was waiting in the kitchen with dinner made and apologies spewing out of his mouth. I just looked at him, and then I looked at my daughter. Reluctantly, once again, I accepted his apology. Life continued. It was such a pattern, a pattern I was too blind to see at that time. Or maybe I did see it, I just wasn't ready to accept it and do anything about it. I don't know."

"So, even after all that," Sarah looked me straight in the eye and asked, "didn't have enough yet, huh?"

"You think I would've, but I still brought him back every time. I didn't know it then, but I was an enabler. When you're an enabler, you can't see it. I don't know why, but you can't for a very long time. Then one day, you just wake up and *poof!* It's all clear, and you can see it plain as day."

"Poof?"

"Yes, just like that—it's all clear! Weirdest thing, but it's true. Guess it's the breaking point where you can see everything clear as day. You see everything that was, and you can envision the future. It's like the sky opened up, the clouds moved away and the sun was shining down warm and bright.

"For me, the 'poof' was the time he physically touched me when he was drunk. It started three days after my parents' twenty-fifth wedding anniversary when we had a huge argument. It was over money. Our biggest fights were always over money. I made more money than he did, and he always wanted to spend. I used to hide the bankbooks and opened a separate account for Courtney that he could not get a hold of. On this particular morning, we fought over the bankbook, which he found. He demanded we go to the bank so he could withdraw money. Defeated, I drove to the bank with him hot on my tail.

Once we reached the bank, we got out of our cars, stood in the middle of the bank parking lot, and screamed at the top of our lungs at each other. Courtney was in the back of the car, crying and wondering what could be going on. Our relationship was so out of control; money was the only thing I could control and that I fought to keep control of."

"Why such a violent argument over money?"

"This may be hard to understand for some, but when you feel like there are so many things you can't control in your life, you hold on tight to those things you know you can. I had a good job and worked hard for what I had been able to accomplish. So, I held tight to the money. I earned it, and I wanted to own it."

"I can see how that makes sense. It was the one thing you controlled in a world of a million things you couldn't."

"That morning, I didn't give up the bankbook. At a break in the screaming, I got in my car, drove away, and cried myself all the way to work thinking about what my life had become in comparison to what I had dreamed my life would be. I was a beautiful young mother with a good job, good health, and a supportive family living in a marriage made in hell. No one knew. I wondered how many other people lived the same secret life, pretending they were living the dream of the perfect relationship. How many individuals are willing to let their soul die just a little each day to hold on to a possible better tomorrow? How many think that maybe tomorrow's promise will be the one that he keeps? Tomorrow, he will realize he doesn't need to drink to be happy—that I can make him happy, *maybe tomorrow*. There were so many dreams of the perfect tomorrows that never came. Each night, I would lay my head on the pillow and dream that tomorrow my love would be enough for him.

"That evening, Kevin didn't come home from work on time—again. It was midnight when he came home with eight of his bar-drinking friends. They were going to have a party at the house. I tried to go to sleep as the party began downstairs. I was afraid at night so I had begun to sleep with a knife under my pillow to protect us. This evening was no different."

"Wait a second. Did I hear you correctly that you said you're sleeping with a knife under your pillow?"

"Yes."

"Things were that frightening?"

"Yes. In my heart, I didn't believe that Kevin would actually hurt us, but he was not consistent in his behavior, and I'd heard enough horrific stories about drunk people who did things they didn't even remember. As a result, my head said, 'Keep the knife close—just in case.'"

"Sorry, I just couldn't believe what you said. Was it like a steak knife or a butcher knife?"

"It was more like a steak knife but a little larger. I was afraid if I kept anything too sharp, I would reach under my pillow in the middle of the night and slice my finger off!"

"Wow. That is very frightening. Please continue. Tell us about this evening. Why was it different?"

"The air was warm on this April day, and after we argued about his planned party and his friends, the friends left. I could tell Kevin was more aggravated than usual that night, so I woke Courtney and held her tight. As he ranted, raved, and screamed at the top of his lungs, he headed to the backyard and stood under our huge pine tree screaming, 'I'm an ass! I hate myself! I hate my life! I'm going to end it all tonight!'

"All I kept thinking was, *Please, Lord, let me just see the sunrise soon.* It was so dark, so very dark and sad at two a.m. I laid Courtney on the couch in the living room so I had her close by.

"As I looked out of the window over the kitchen sink, I could see him turn and head back to the house. I backed into the dining room as he entered from the breezeway and stood there frozen as I watched him grab the largest butcher knife from our kitchen counter block and say, 'It is time to die.' For a moment, I thought he was going to stab me. Instead, he ordered us out of the house.

"I remember screaming, 'Screw you! I'm not leaving this house!' We stood in the kitchen for what seemed like hours yelling at each other. After about ten minutes, he put the knife down and I thought that he was going to calm down and walk away. Instead, he took three steps towards the back door but then whipped around quickly, ran towards me, grabbed me by the arms, dug his nails into the skin of my upper arms, and threw me against the wall by the cellar stairs. As quickly as my head slammed into the door frame, I could feel a bump emerge. It was the first and last time he ever physically hurt me. I knew right then that I was right. This was a night that would be like no other and one of us or all of us could die. His anger and drinking had reached new heights. I think he was even a little surprised that he had thrown me as he grabbed the knife and headed back outside."

"I'm in shock. How did you stay focused?"

"I had to protect my baby. Courtney didn't deserve this. She didn't ask for this. She was just a little innocent angel that I loved with all my heart."

"What'd you do?"

"I grabbed the phone and Courtney, locked us inside a small dining room closet for safety, and called '911' for help. It was probably not the smartest place to hide since you could see the phone cord running along the wall, but it was the first place I could think of and at least I could brace myself against the door frame to hold the door shut and lock us in. Once I placed the call, the dispatcher said to get out of the house. 'Cops are on their way.'

"Slowly, I opened the door a crack and peered outside to see where Kevin was. He wasn't nearby, so I slowly exited the closet and peered around the corner into the kitchen to see him standing in the breezeway between the house and the garage. With Courtney wrapped in my arms, I ran out the front door and stood by the big maple tree at the corner of the driveway and road. Kevin must have heard the front door close because within minutes, he walked back from the breezeway into the house. I could see him walk room to room as he turned on and off the lights. I don't know if he was looking for us. Within minutes, he was at the front dining room window peering directly out at me across the front lawn. He had found us. He lifted the window, stuck his head outside, and screamed, 'This is for you!' I stood there and watched motionless and helpless as he slit both of his wrists and screamed, 'It's time to die!'

"I hoped he would die right there, and I knew as those thoughts were racing through my head that they were not the Christian thoughts to have. I was probably going to hell for thinking it, but I didn't care. I couldn't take it any longer. I couldn't live like this. I wanted him to end it for all of us. Then, as quickly as that thought came, it went. As I looked at my beautiful daughter sitting next to me watching what just unfolded before us, I thought, *He can't die. That's not fair. That's the chicken's way out and it's too easy for him.*

"Although it seemed like an hour, the police swarmed the neighborhood within minutes. When I say swarmed, I mean they were *everywhere*. There were four cruisers with lights and sirens blaring as they raced down the street to my house. They screeched to a halt in front, and two officers ensured I was OK before focusing their attention on

Kevin. After coaxing him to put the knife down, they walked him out the door and into the waiting ambulance. He sat on the back of the ambulance as they took a look at his wrists and wrapped the wounds with temporary bandages to stop the bleeding. I was mortified, not just because of the humiliation I felt, but also because the whole neighborhood had just witnessed a peek into my secret life. How could I ever face them? I just wanted to crawl under a rock and hide, pack my bags, move, and never look back. *Never* in my wildest dreams could I ever fathom that this was what my life would come to. I was in my early twenties. My life was falling apart.

"The police asked two questions: Did I want to press charges for domestic violence? Did he hit me? I hesitated and then answered no to both. After they took him away to the hospital, I went back into the house and cleaned up the blood just like I had so many times before. I rocked Courtney to sleep, bowed my head, and once again asked God for strength and guidance. Then I cried and cried until there were no more tears left to cry. I fell asleep for a short time in the rocking chair holding Courtney tight. It was the morning light against my face that woke me to the new day."

"That was your perfect time to tell the police that he touched you. It would have set you free. Why didn't you do it?"

"I almost did. I thought about it. I double thought about it. But I couldn't. He was so sad. I thought, *How can I send him to jail when he has so many major issues?* So I didn't tell the cops.

"After he left, my second thought was, *Why couldn't he cut himself deep enough to hurt himself?* Seriously, I was sort of pissed that he couldn't even kill himself right.

"Kevin had been taken to the hospital. I didn't know who to tell. My parents were in the Bahamas celebrating their twenty-fifth wedding anniversary. No one in my family knew what I was going through, and

I didn't have the strength yet to tell them. I knew my sister would be there for me, and I knew I could call my best girlfriend, but I was too embarrassed to call either. I had no one."

"But you called somebody, didn't you? Tell us what you did."

"As I mentioned, I awoke to the light of the sun shining into the room still sitting in that rocking chair with my daughter sleeping on my lap. As I was feeding Courtney breakfast, I thought hard about what I would do. I grabbed the phone and called the one person I thought should help to fix the mess that was created."

"Who'd you call?"

"Kevin's mother."

"You did? Why her?"

"She raised him and she screwed him up. I told her she needed to get to the hospital immediately, to go take care of her son because I was so tired of it. I couldn't take it any longer. It was her turn."

"Why would you think she screwed him up?"

Silently, I thought for a moment about why she was responsible. "At that time, I figured she must not have been a great mother to him. That somehow her parenting was responsible for his choices. I was angry and upset and I felt she should take some responsibility for his actions. I had no one else that I was willing to tell. I surely wasn't ready to call my family."

"What did she say?"

"At first, she said nothing. I think she was in shock, shock that I was talking to her like I was and also shocked that Kevin had slit his wrists.

Not sure what shocked her more. I'm sure she was probably mortified and angry. But she heard me and got into her car and drove to the hospital. Courtney and I went a few hours later. I thought about not going—just leaving him there—but there was something in me that wasn't ready to walk away yet. He needed me. He had issues. I wasn't going to leave him. Gosh, I sound like my own broken record. I can hear it now; too bad I couldn't hear it then. I couldn't see what this was doing to Courtney and me. I just had to stand by my man. That's what I did. He was observed, referred to a counselor to call for an appointment based on the fact that he might be suicidal, and was sent home. And so, the cycle continued.

"So that day, two new people joined our secret party of lies. I was too embarrassed to tell anyone else. It was my own little secret that I kept buried deep inside of my soul—where it was eating away at the fiber of who I was. Anyone who has ever been in such a situation understands the true embarrassment that goes along with someone's drinking habit and abusiveness. You are treated as if you were at fault, and eventually, when you are in that situation long enough, you are brainwashed to believe it. If you're beat down enough to think it's you that's not worthy, you begin to believe that. It's the conflict between emotions and logical thought. You can't break away because you're so convinced that you leaving the person will drive them to make worse choices and it will be your fault.

"He went to counseling for a while. There were times I also went to counseling both for myself and also with him. So that no one knew that I was going to counseling, I went during work. Going during work was tough, since the sessions almost always ended in tears and going back to work with red eyes was a dead giveaway something was wrong. If I could, I would make an excuse that I had a meeting later in the afternoon and went right after work. Things with us were good for a few months, and then they turned bad again. The anger, drinking binges, and now violent acts began again. I guess I never realized, or maybe I chose to selectively ignore, the signs of how dangerous the relationship was becoming."

"What made you realize that things were not going to improve?"

"The day everything changed was the day his counselor called me and said that either he or I or both of us were going to be hurt or killed and I needed to walk away, to get out. That was the day I fully realized the potential impact on our lives. The realization was that keeping the family unit together was not in the best interest of anyone."

"Did you walk that day?"

"Not quite. I know, you're probably thinking I was crazy not to pack my bags and just run. I didn't, but I did know what I had to do. I just needed to find the time when it was right. So, I put together a plan of action on how I was going to position myself and prepare for the day to leave when it came. I jotted down high-level items just to start to wrap my head around a plan. Didn't know if it'd be in a day, a month, or a year, but I knew this was not the life I wanted to lead and that day would come.

"I had something I could control again—in a world where everything was spinning out of control, I had something."

"I'm not sure I understand. Your life is spinning. What can you control?"

"On that day, I found the clarity that I could control my future. I could plan my next steps. I could get out of the relationship. I owned my actions. I owned something. I could be in charge."

"When was it right?"

"When was it the right time to leave? Turned out it was a few months later.

"The morning I left started like so many others—getting ready for work and getting Courtney ready for my mom's. Kevin started an argument. I can't even remember over what. It escalated into a fight over money—once again—the control point of our relationship. He followed my car, bumping into the back at stop signs until I pulled into the local grocery store parking lot. He was threatening to take all the money out of the account. This time, unlike so many other times, I just handed over the bankbook to him. *Fuck you*, I thought, *I'm done.* I didn't care any longer. It wasn't important any longer. The one thing I fought to control, I gave away. I was defeated. I drove away. He had the money."

"That was such a control point for you for so many years. You left with nothing."

"On that morning, I didn't see it that way. In the past, I had, but that morning, I left with peace of mind. For me, that was all I needed. I could rebuild the rest."

"So that was your 'poof'?"

"Yes. Just like that. I was done. It was that simple. A calming force surrounded my body, and I knew what I had to do. There were no tears. I just had an action plan. I walked into my parents' house to drop off Courtney and simply stated to my parents that I had had enough. My marriage was over, and I was filing for divorce. They hugged me and said they would stand beside me on whatever decision I made, and then they told me they loved me.

"Off to work I drove. When I got to the office, I took out a pad of paper where I had started to write down everything I needed to do to move on with my life and take control. It was my finest to-do list ever! I didn't say anything when I got home that day or the next few days as I began to execute the items on my list. I moved money from bank accounts. See, he never took the money out even though he had threatened to. So, the accounts were intact. I set up my beneficiary at work to be Courtney and checked the cost for benefit coverage on my own plans. I had an exit plan, and I was taking baby steps. One step at a time, I was walking toward my new life. I was controlling my life. Kevin didn't know what my plans were, but I did.

"A few days later, Kevin and I had to carpool to work. His truck was in the shop. On the way home, we picked up Courtney and then began the ten-minute drive home. The car was the safest place I could think of, so as we pulled up the street from my parents, I took a deep breath and told him I was done. I was done with his drinking, the fighting, everything. It was not the life I wanted or the life a child should be raised in. I was filing for divorce. Just like that. No tears. No emotion. I was calm and matter of fact. I didn't have anything left in me. My fight was gone. He had sucked the life out of me and any remaining tears. I was dry. He asked that I pull the car over. I did, and he said he was going to walk back to our house; he needed time to think…So, I pulled over, let him out, and drove home. I could breathe. It felt good."

"Were you scared that he might explode?"

"Part of me worried about that, but I still felt good, and even if he did go off, I had people who knew now. I had my support. I was moving in the right direction. So, I made dinner and waited for him to get home.

"It was dark when he got home. It was five hours later. He staggered up the stairs—drunk."

"Drunk?"

"Yes, wasted. At that moment, I knew without any shred of doubt that I had made the right choice. He begged and pleaded with me not to file, to give him another chance, to work at our marriage."

"And you said…?"

"'No. Are you serious? You came home drunk!' I was done-done. There was nothing left to discuss."

"No emotion?"

"No. I was at my end. People fight because they care. They're fighting for something they want. When the fight is over, it's because there's nothing left to fight for. There was no fight left in me. I had become an empty shell.

"For the first time in a very long time, I slept soundly that evening with the knife tucked under my pillow and the phone on my nightstand. He slept downstairs. I would no longer enable him. Step one in a long journey. I was proud. I took step one.

"The next day, I went to the lawyer across the street from my office at work, put down the financial retainer, and filed the papers. I felt liberated and sad—both at the same time. He was served seven days later, January 1991. I made the decision that I would never embarrass him and allowed him to arrange a mutually agreeable location with the sheriff. Regardless of what he had done to me, I would not disrespect him. He moved out of the house to a rented room within a month. During that time, we drove Courtney back and forth so he could see her two days a week. She never slept over at his apartment; she was too young."

"Wow. I can only imagine the emotions going through you as he began to prepare to move out."

"It was the toughest thing I had to do, but I think it was the right move. To this day, I still believe it was the right thing to do."

"Let's take a commercial break. We'll be back in five minutes. Let's get some water over here for our guest."

With cameras off, Sarah asked how I was holding up.

"I'm doing OK. The tough part is yet to come. Can you have someone bring out a box of tissues? I'll just stuff them under my chair in case I need them."

"Of course. You're doing great. The audience is mesmerized. People can relate to what you've been through. Take a few minutes and really look out at our guests before we are back on the air. They are talking amongst themselves and absorbing what they are learning about your experiences. I am sure more than a few of them are able to relate."

As I scanned the audience, my eyes caught a group of women to the right of the stage who had stepped out of their seats and walked to the aisle. They seemed to be surrounding a young lady, maybe around twenty. Two women of the group had their arms around her, like a mother would shelter a child. *Is she suffering in an abusive relationship? Does she know someone who is?* I saw one of the women pull a tissue from her grey clutch purse and gently wipe the tear from the red-headed young lady's eyes. *She is very lucky to have friends who are comforting her. I hope she takes something away from my experience.* I watched as they hugged each other and returned to their seats. *I will never know what that discussion entailed, but I am imagining it is positive.*

It seemed like twenty minutes later when I was snapped back to reality with Sarah turning to me as the director shouted that we had two minutes left in the break.

"Ready?"

With a smile, I replied, "Yes, I am."

"Tell us what life was like after you made the decision and filed for divorce."

"Kevin was gone. I promised myself that I would never ever put myself in an abusive relationship again. I would put myself, my daughter, and our lives front and center for any decision I made. During the time he was gone, I received a promotion at work and was feeling quite good about myself. Things were going really well. I was happy, really happy for the first time in a very long time."

Chapter 4

Kevin, Round Two

"Life settled into a new routine, and we were OK on our own. There wasn't fear in the home; no one had to walk on eggshells. There was peace. For the first time in many years, Kevin began to take care of himself. He lost fifty pounds, ate healthy, attended counseling sessions regularly, and stopped drinking. He was a new man…and slowly and unexpectedly, I fell in love with the Kevin I had met years earlier."

"Are you saying you started dating again?"

"Yes. We went out on a few dates, and then we started to hang out with Courtney as a family. I was still physically attracted to him, and before we knew it, all the old feelings were back again.

"Soon, he moved back into our home, and I stopped the divorce proceedings. He had been gone for six months. I thought long and hard about that decision because I knew I was placing a lot of trust into a relationship that had caused me a lot of hurt and pain. I also knew that I had to let go of the anger and had to accept what had occurred as being in the past—not to be brought up in discussions and arguments when it was convenient. I knew I could forgive him for what we had gone through, but I wasn't sure I could ever really forget or that I would want to forget what I went through. I never wanted to feel what I felt then again. *Ever*!

"As hard as it was to file for divorce and walk away from the relationship initially, I felt strongly that we needed to give our marriage another chance. We had a daughter who deserved both parents together and happy if that was possible. I didn't believe in divorce. I believed you made a commitment and you stuck with it. I took those vows 'good times and bad' seriously when I stood in front of my family and God.

"You're looking at me like you think I was crazy for taking him back. Is that what's racing through your head right now—words like *crazy, insane, nuts?*"

"Yes. I'm thinking you're crazy! It was very risky on your part. With that said, however, I understand your strong belief in the unity of family, your daughter's need for two parents, and, as you saw him change for the better, a second chance. Not sure I'd allow him another chance, but I haven't been in your shoes, so I can't say. So, we're all wondering what happened. Tell us, how'd it go?"

"Together, we built a relationship based on love, trust, and mutual respect. Although I can say that I never forgot what we went through, I did forgive. He didn't drink for the next ten years, and we had a solid, loving relationship. We did family events, went on family vacations, and were very happy. It was wonderful. My parents were happy to see us back together. My mother was extremely pleased as I think for her she felt it was the best arrangement for our daughter. I think for my dad, he was happy because I was happy. He would have been absolutely supportive of me whether we got back together or not.

"No regrets. I truly believe everything happens for a reason. I think we can agree that when you're in the midst of something bad, you can't always see what that reason might be at the time. In the future, you are given the wisdom and opportunity to stop and do a twenty-twenty look back. That's when you can usually see it.

"The heads are shaking all over the audience in disbelief that I took him back. I think the whole audience thinks I've just made the biggest mistake, huh? Is everyone thinking that I'm crazy right now? Let me give you a little view into my twenty-twenty hindsight perspective on why this chance was well worth it. Here goes. You ready?"

"Yes. Tell us"

"About a year into this renewed relationship, we got pregnant. Well, I actually got pregnant; Kevin helped. We told everyone immediately because we had such a simple first pregnancy. The family was so excited. It was a beautiful summer Sunday when Courtney, Mom, and I went out strawberry picking like we had done so many summers before. When we were done, we headed back to Mom's house to drop off the berries, and when I went to the bathroom to pee, I noticed I had started bleeding. I was shocked and drove home immediately to call my doctor's office. They had me gauge the amount of blood and told me to lie on my back with my legs elevated and the bleeding should stop. They reassured me that this could happen and not to worry. In my heart, I already knew there was a problem based on Courtney's simple and uneventful pregnancy. I knew my body. The day dragged by as the bleeding increased, and late into the night, the cramping began and we headed to the hospital. After the examination, the doctor said we had a fifty-fifty chance that the pregnancy would abort. I was so sad and cried all the way home. I headed right to bed with pillows propped up under my legs.

"The next morning, the bleeding continued and the cramping was much worse. It was around nine when I asked Kevin to bring Courtney to my parents. She did not need to see me in this agony. The stomach cramps continued to worsen by the hour, and by eleven o'clock, I was sitting on the toilet doubled over in pain. I called my doctor to discuss the symptoms. After our brief discussion, she confirmed my fears. I was going to lose the baby. It was no longer 'if' but rather 'when.' The doctor instructed me to remain seated on the toilet and when the fetus discharged, to scoop it, place it in a container, and bring it to the office."

"She said what?"

"Yes. I know. I was like, *what?* What did you say to do? Scoop out the baby?"

"That was the instruction? That's horrible."

"Yes. I couldn't believe I had to do this. Even telling the story almost twenty years later, I get all emotional. It was a very sad and painful thing to go through. Look at my hands; they still shake when I think of that day. I can still feel the abdominal pains. I was supposed to have a healthy pregnancy and deliver a beautiful baby, not pull a fetus from the toilet. *What the hell was that?* How cruel life can be sometimes. It was just before noon on that Sunday when I was doubled over on the toilet having full-blown birthing contractions and Kevin was searching frantically through the cabinets for a Tupperware container with a lid and a slotted spoon. It was about an hour of intense cramps when I felt the fetus pass. Felt like a giant blood clot and created a splash in the toilet bowl. I sat there for another twenty minutes or so until the cramping subsided with my face cradled in my hands and crying. I cried for the loss of a baby, for the loss of a life, the loss of a dream, and for the physical pain. I just cried until there were no more tears.

"When I finally composed myself, I wiped the blood away, put on a maxi pad, and pulled up my panties. With the Tupperware in my left hand, I fished out the fetus from the deeply blood-stained toilet with the slotted spoon in my right hand, threw the toilet paper in, and flushed it all away. Kevin and I drove hand in hand in silence to the doctor's office and entered a waiting area full of beautifully pregnant women with their giant stomachs and their loving significant others, glowing at the impending birth of their babies. There we were in the corner by the fish tank with a Tupperware container on my lap and the baby I would never have floating inside. As I sat quietly wrapped in the loving arms of my husband with tears gently rolling down my cheeks, I wondered why."

"What an extremely emotional day. You must've been just devastated."

"Yes, I was. Besides the sadness, all I was thinking was *can someone just throw me a bone*—make things easy for me for just a little while? Give me a break! Didn't we deserve some happiness for the challenges we'd experienced?

"The fetus was sent to the lab for testing to ensure there was nothing genetic that we should be concerned with. The doctor said we should try to get pregnant right away. I looked at Kevin as he held me gently and sadly said, 'No.' In two days, my dreams of a second child were gone and I was not able to comprehend the ability to just move on. It wasn't so simple to just get pregnant again.

"We were at the end of the thirteenth week. We should have been home free—past the twelve-week mark. It was not to be. Father's Day 1992 will be remembered as the day we lost our second child. Starting that day, when asked how many pregnancies I'd had, I would say two pregnancies and one child.

"I never realized how difficult it was when someone had a miscarriage. I never realized how you become attached to this life within you, a life you don't even know."

Sarah turned to the audience. "Has anyone here lost a baby?"

As the hands were raised in the audience, I could see the tears in the eyes of women who had dreamed of motherhood but were not granted that dream. I sat there and thought that probably some tried again and completed successful pregnancies, but in the tears of many, I could still see that the dream had not yet been realized.

"Over the next few days, Kevin and I mourned by ourselves and together, and this experience brought us closer and created a stronger bond. I took a whole week off from work and cried. All the clothes that we had begun to pull out and organize were all boxed back up, put back into the closet. I was not to be a mother again. At least not right now.

"Courtney was almost four at this time, and we discussed not having any more children. I could not imagine going through another miscarriage. Only those who have miscarried can fully appreciate the sense of loss. It was so much more overwhelming than I had ever expected. I didn't think too much about how the woman felt when I learned of someone who had had a miscarriage. My perspective was changed forever based on my experience.

"Kevin didn't mind if we didn't have more children. We both felt blessed with Courtney and decided to proceed with having a vasectomy since he felt that it was something he could do. Based on all that I had been through, going through a surgery was not something he wanted me to have to do. A few months after the miscarriage, we went to the first appointment, which was to discuss the procedure and fully understand the implications. It was not reversible. It was permanent. After discussing further at home, we decided to proceed. Courtney would be an only child. We would spoil her, and she would be fine with it. We scheduled the appointment to have the surgery done.

"Around ten days before the surgery date, for a reason we didn't understand at that time, we decided not to go through with the procedure. Both of us had the same thought at almost the same time. One day at dinner, we simultaneously raised concerns about going through with surgery. The next day, we cancelled it. We didn't plan to get pregnant again and were careful to prevent it."

"But something different happened?"

"Yes. Someone had different plans for us. June 1993, I found out I was three months pregnant. The day I took the pregnancy test was Father's Day. It was wonderful since the prior year's Father's Day was so sad. Our child was due on or around Christmas—anywhere from five days before to five days after. I just hoped it wasn't Christmas morning. This was Courtney's five-year-old Christmas. Santa was delivering the two-wheel bike. I didn't want her to wake up without Mom and Dad there to celebrate with her. It was a really big Christmas for her.

"My pregnancy was picture perfect, and I was beautiful, amazing, and glowing. I had only gained around twenty-five pounds and most of it was baby. I held my breath until after the first ultrasound, and you could see the baby actively moving. I knew we would have a baby this time. The whole family was convinced that I was having a boy based on how I was carrying. We even purchased boy clothes!"

Sarah turned to me and asked, "The room was painted and everything was ready for the baby? Did you pick out names as well?"

"We knew if it was a boy, he would be named Jonathon Robert after our fathers. Since we were convinced it was a boy, there was no need to think about a girl name. So, we didn't."

"How was Kevin during this pregnancy?"

"He was wonderful. This pregnancy was a very different experience than the last. We were a family, and it was great, everything I had hoped for. We still periodically fought about stupid things, but we had learned to talk things out and find compromise in situations.

"After nine wonderful months, it was around four Christmas morning when I was awakened by contractions. I ignored them, figuring they were Braxton-Hicks, just like I had experienced on so many other occasions. It was around six when I couldn't breathe through them any longer and we put our plans in action. Kevin called my sister to get to the house and then called Mom to let her know we would be picking her up shortly. She was at Courtney's birth and of course, would be at her second grandchild's birth. It was a beautiful Christmas morning with a small amount of snow on the roads that made the streets glisten as we drove to the hospital.

"We arrived around seven, and we exited our car in the underground parking lot to walk toward the emergency room. We couldn't have walked twenty feet when we heard a large bang. We turned around to see our car being hit by a drunk driver's pickup truck. It hit the passenger-side door. Had I still been in the car we could only imagine what would have happened to me. We entered the hospital and asked that they call the police. The nurse asked if I wanted to go upstairs, but I decided to hang out and wait for the police in the lobby. I knew that as soon as I went upstairs, they would start poking and prodding and all the students would be measuring my vagina. I was waiting downstairs comfortably perched in my wheelchair watching the police do their job. Around seven forty-five, the police report was completed and they wheeled me up—not a moment too soon. I was having severe challenges breathing through the contractions. As soon as I got out of my clothes and into the lovely gown, with my butt hanging out of course, my water broke all over the bathroom floor. I made my way to the bed and had my vagina measured—fully dilated and fully effaced. The baby was coming. I was wheeled down to delivery with my mom and husband in tow. A couple of pushes and our baby was born."

"A boy?"

"No. The doctor said it was a girl. We were so convinced she was a boy, that when the doctor announced it was a girl, we asked that he double-check. It was a girl. She was beautiful, and we couldn't be happier. Chloe Amber Towers was welcomed into our family.

"We called Courtney to let her know she had a sister. Her response was, "Good. If it was a brother it couldn't come home." We took a few family pictures with our Santa hats on, and I sent Kevin and Mom on their way back home to make Christmas a fun day for big sister Courtney. Because of the car accident, they could only take right turns all the way home, so getting home took a little longer than normal. By the time they arrived, Courtney had opened every present under the tree. We didn't mind. Courtney was so happy. In the evening, she came to visit us in the hospital. Thank God it wasn't a boy; I would have had one disappointed daughter!

"Chloe was truly a miracle baby, a testament to the difficulty we had endured and the bond that kept us together. She made our family complete, and we felt on top of the world. We had the relationship I had always wanted, full of love. We did things together as a family. I was truly happy in my marriage for the first time."

"Any more baby plans?"

"No. Kevin did have the vasectomy about two weeks before Chloe was born, because we knew that even if there was anything wrong with the delivery, we would not have any additional children just based on the age difference between the girls."

"That was quite a roller-coaster ride over two years."

"Yes, it was. We don't know why things happen until much later, and sometimes you just need to believe that the choices that are made will lead down the right trail. So, as I mentioned, this was my twenty-twenty reflection, and it showed a really cool path that we could've never seen standing at the beginning of it!

"To summarize: if I didn't find the strength to file for divorce, Kevin wouldn't have taken care of himself, we wouldn't have gotten back together, and if we didn't cancel the vasectomy, I wouldn't have had my Chloe."

"That's amazing when you see how it weaves together."

"I know. The path of the decisions led us to a great point in our lives."

"So things were pretty normal for many years?"

"Yes, we were a good, solid family, and the girls had a great relationship with both their father and me. As I mentioned earlier, we had a great ten years. So you're probably wondering when things started to go downhill again."

"Hold on; before we go down that path, I'm getting flagged that we need a commercial break. Be back in five minutes."

Sarah turned to me. "There are a lot of personal details of your life that you are sharing. I can tell the audience is very engaged in the discussion. Are you OK, Stephanie?"

"Yes. Being here and sharing is the right decision. Looks like we're getting flagged that the quick break is over. Let me reapply my lipstick quickly before the bright lights go back on, if you don't mind."

"No problem, you have about 30 seconds.

"OK, we're back. So, it's ten great years. What made you think things were starting to degrade?"

"Fast forward six years to 1999. It was this fall when I noticed that Kevin was acting weird, shutting down, keeping his distance, maybe starting to get depressed again? I wasn't sure. I started to make notes on his behavior in my diary, trying to find patterns in what was going on and what may have been triggering his behavior."

"You kept a diary?"

"Yes, I kept a diary throughout this whole experience; it was my sanity check. It was a way for me to write what I was feeling where no one would ask questions. It was just my private world.

"I thought he was having an affair. Couldn't understand why he would, but I had the thoughts in my head. I would ask him, and he would say no. He had been a good dad and husband over the last ten years, but I noted some things that stood out as very different behavior. I was worried."

"Give us some examples of what you mean as different or weird behavior."

"OK. Here are some items: he wouldn't build the kids a skating rink in the backyard, stopped sleeping with me and began sleeping on the couch, didn't attend the girls' concert but stayed home to do lawn work, was not eating dinner with us, refused to let Courtney get a bunny so I had my dad build a bunny cage and I bought her the bunny anyway…things that were no longer family-focused. I considered it weird behavior."

"Yes. Seems a little odd."

"I couldn't understand why it was about him now and not about the girls or the family. I knew something was up, but when someone won't talk about it, what do you do?"

"He wouldn't talk so it sounds like you began to learn to live around it."

"You're absolutely right. It's amazing what women, and I'm sure some men, put up with in relationships. And so, I adjusted.

"The following June, despite whatever was going on with Kevin, we moved into our 'dream house.' For many, it would not be the mansion they dreamed of, but to me, I felt like I had arrived. I had two beautiful daughters, a two-thousand-square-foot colonial home with three bedrooms, three baths, two living rooms, a kitchen, and a dining room on almost an acre of land. We installed a pool and clubhouse and put up a basketball hoop for the girls. We had our dog, Spike, in the backyard and a guinea pig named Toaster in the bedroom upstairs. Everything from the outside was perfect. We had a beautiful home and the perfect life. We were living the American dream."

"Was it really the perfect life on the inside of the house?"

"Not 100 percent exactly. Remember, there is truly no American dream. It was tolerable, but things began to move in the wrong direction.

"Even though the home life was starting to become difficult, my career was going well. My career was always important to me; it gave me a level of confidence that I needed to feel valued since I wasn't feeling valued at home. Over the years, I had to work harder and longer hours, and with Kevin beginning to act weird, I decided that maybe my career was creating issues in my marriage. I was thinking that perhaps I was spending too much time and energy at work and traveling, so I decided to step down from my high-stress job and become an individual contributor, going to a project manager role, part-time, working thirty hours a week. I thought it would help me find balance in my life and strengthen our marriage. Part of how I defined myself was how successful I was at work and how much money I made. Remember the bankbook fights we had at the bank parking lot? This was a huge decision for me. Stepping down felt a little like failure and defeat because it showed that I couldn't do it all. I had to make a choice, and I was OK with that. I chose my marriage."

"Did you regret your choice of changing jobs after you made it?"

"No. It was the right thing to do at that time. I was able to spend more time with the girls and spend time volunteering for school activities, like coaching cheerleading, running fundraisers, coordinating a gift certificate program, and running the school auction. I put my girls and my family first, and I was happy."

"Did it enhance and improve your marriage?"

"Unfortunately, even that major life change didn't accomplish what I hoped. It didn't strengthen my marriage."

"So, you're in your dream home and you've made changes in your work to find more balance. You're happier with your choices, but your marriage is not getting any better?"

"Yes. Unfortunately, the marriage was the same. A few months after we moved in, out of the blue one evening, Kevin just stated that he didn't care any longer…about anything! I thought that was a very strange statement. What would that mean to all of us? He wouldn't elaborate. It was a very random statement. He said things like that every now and then."

"Did he ever elaborate?"

"No. I didn't know it yet, but it was an indicator of what was coming."

Chapter 5

Distance and Death

"The following year, 2001, Kevin became even more distant from the girls and me. Sometimes he was very much engaged with the family, and other times, he would find excuses to leave rooms we were in or not attend things we were doing as a family. His mood swings were intense, and it was really tough to continuously walk on eggshells. Watching every word I said and how it could trigger some negative reaction was rough. We had a family vacation planned in October to Disney World so I decided I was going to hang on until we had our fun vacation and through the holidays to make sure the girls had a good time. Then, I knew I was going to have to confront his behavior."

"How did you feel during this time?"

"I was sad and frustrated. I didn't know what was going on. I'd noticed he had started to put chewing tobacco in his cheeks. It's gross. He still wasn't sleeping with me. I missed having someone to snuggle with at bedtime. There were no hugs or kisses, and I felt sadder and sadder every day. I didn't understand why he didn't want all the love I could give. I would think to myself, *I'm a good mom and good friend and wife to Kevin, so I don't understand why he doesn't love me more.* It was at this time that I realized that I wasn't going to make my goal of retiring at the age of forty. I needed to ensure I could support the girls and me financially if anything happened to my marriage.

Stepping away from my job would not be in the best interests of any of us. I was focusing on the kids, giving them the most I could. I was not happy with my life."

"You described yourself as a good mom and a good friend and wife. You don't use the word *lover*."

"Unfortunately, that's because we weren't. There wasn't that intense passion, that desire to be with each other. No desire to hold, to kiss, to love. He didn't want me. Or maybe he didn't know how to love me the way I wanted or needed to be loved. Kevin and I became roommates. We were not lovers; we were not life partners. It's a sad day when you realize your dreams will not be fulfilled and you have to decide what you're willing to accept to find minimal happiness. The thoughts you begin to ponder are around how much you are willing to settle for so that you keep the family intact."

"You made a choice?"

"Yes. It was a choice, and I knew exactly what I was doing. I chose to forego my happiness to keep the family together and give the girls the stability they needed. I learned how to accept and find joy in little things that didn't include my husband. Once I made my decision, I made the best of it.

"Toward the end of the year, Kevin received a call from his mother, Anna. He hadn't spoken to her in about eight years, and he had always said that the next time he spoke to her it would probably be because she was dying. Unfortunately, his casual comment became something more. She said she had pneumonia and was in and out of the hospital. We learned shortly after our first visit at the hospital that unfortunately, she had lung cancer. He was right. She was dying."

"So, he hasn't seen her in years, gets a call out of the blue, and has to accept the fact that she is dying?"

"Yes. That was a very tough day. Actually, it was a tough year."

"How'd it affect you both?"

"I never watched someone die before, and this was a very difficult period in our lives. The situation added stress to an already struggling marriage. Kevin spent time with his mother and saw her at least every few weeks. It was about a year later in the fall of 2002 that she began to deteriorate quickly. She lost a lot of weight, and her lungs were beginning to fill with fluids.

"The last few weeks, she was in hospice at the hospital. We were there frequently, and toward the end of her life, we were there daily. During her last week, we were there immediately after work each day. Kevin stayed late into the night and only left to go home and sleep for a few hours. It was very sad to watch her deterioration—she went from actively speaking and eating to a coma four days later. Anna told my mother that she would not die with Kevin in the room, and during one of her last conscious days, she asked me to come close to the bed so she could talk to me. I walked to the edge of the bed and took her hand in mine. She looked me square in the eye and asked me to promise to take good care of Kevin forever."

"She had no idea what was going on, huh?"

"No. I thought to myself, *You have got to be kidding me. Figures I would be asked to make a promise I can't keep for a woman's dying wish.* I took a slow, steady breath in as I stood at her hospital bed looking at her very frail and tiny body. Her hair had thinned to nothing and her glasses engulfed her frail face. I chose my words very carefully before I spoke. I knew that there were challenges in our marriage and that was a promise I could not keep."

"How did you respond?"

"I said I would support him as best I could. That I meant.

"The last day, her breathing became very difficult, and with every breath in, we waited to see if she would exhale. You could hear the liquid in her lungs, which is referred to as the death gurgle. You could smell death. That's why I hate hospitals. It was seven that last night when we left. We had only one car, since the other was in the shop for repairs. I brought Kevin home, and Chloe and I headed to the store to pick up his new suit in preparation for the impending funeral. It's weird because we all know we're going to die at some point, but you're never ever really ready for it. Buying a suit to wear to the funeral of your mother is very upsetting. I had a bad feeling that this may be the night.

"When we returned home about an hour later, the house was lit up like a Christmas tree and we could see that Kevin was standing on the front porch. He was just standing there. I turned to Chloe and muttered, 'This doesn't look good.'

"As soon as we got close to the house, I knew. I just knew his mother had died. He confirmed this as soon as I got out of the truck, and he immediately jumped in and headed back to the hospital to say good-bye before they took the body away.

"I knew that as I watched the truck drive down the street, we were going to be entering an even more challenging time in our marriage. I wondered as I looked at the taillights if he was strong enough to handle what he had to face, including all of the guilt he had stored inside for the years he did not spend with his mother. The fact that his parents lived five miles away from us and didn't even know their grandchildren was a hard reality to accept. He had a closet full of wouldas, couldas, and shouldas. I was generally concerned that he was not strong enough to take this on."

"I can imagine what was going through your head."

"Yeah, it was like looking into the future and knowing that everything that we had worked through to make better was about to drive off the proverbial cliff. At that moment, I thought I had an inkling as to how the death would affect us, but in reality, I had no idea how profound an impact his mother's death would have. Soon, we found out."

"It was tough for him?"

"Yes, tough was an understatement. The guilt of the years they didn't spend together was overwhelming him. My biggest fear was that this would trigger him to start drinking again, and then our lives would become a living hell. We were already not in a great place, so this would most likely add to the challenges. It can't be better. It's going to be worse. Not something I thought I could deal with. I was fearing every day that that would be the day he started to drink. I already knew something was going on in his head based on his behavior. I just didn't know what."

"Did he start drinking again?"

"No. He didn't pick up another drink. He learned to substitute other pleasures to ease his pain. I knew that this was a tough time for him. It would be a difficult time for anyone who lost a parent. Let's flash forward seven months after Anna passed away. Kevin was still not able to deal with the guilt and remorse he was feeling. We were paying the price as a family; he was more distant and not involved in our family activities. He was taking five to six sleeping pills a night to get to sleep, and his bed was the couch.

"Twice during those seven months, Kevin had taken a week off of work, just because he felt like calling in sick. He would just wake up and decide not to go to work. I was busting my ass at work to keep our finances straight. His work ethic was really bothering me because it was not something I would do in my job and it was not the type of behavior I wanted to teach the girls. At this point, I had returned to a full time management position, but controlled the number of hours I spent at work. I never wanted the girls to think it was OK to just walk away from work when the going got tough or they didn't feel like it. Kids need to learn how to deal with the difficult things life throws their way—and this was not the lesson they were learning. It made me both angry and sad."

"Is there any family interaction?"

"No, not really. At this point, he was clearly getting depressed again, and he wouldn't get help. He was not eating dinner with us, not spending a lot of time playing games or talking with the girls. I got sad because he was saying things like 'Just kick me out before you find my body shot.' He was that depressed, but yet, he was not willing to get help to deal with his issues. I didn't understand why keeping us together as a family wasn't more important to him. I knew that I would do everything I possibly could to keep us together and could not comprehend his actions. So, life went on around him—without him.

"Every year for about fifteen years, my family and I rented a beach house during the summer on Wells Beach, Maine. We were all planning to go again this summer, and the girls were very much looking forward to it. Kevin said he didn't think he wanted to go for the whole week and we should take two cars."

"Two cars? That's a strange request."

"Yes. I thought, *Hell no! This is our family vacation, and we need to behave as a family.* After much debate and discussion, we did take one car to Maine and Kevin did spend the whole week. However, he was very nervous, always moving and doing something. Kept saying how much he wanted to get back home."

"That is very weird behavior. Did you ask him to go to counseling when he was acting like that?"

"Begged him daily to not be so selfish and to open his eyes to see what his behavior was doing to our family. He would not do it."

"You must've been thinking *Not again?*"

"I was so upset. All I could think was, *You've got to be kidding me!* Now we had two beautiful young girls who absolutely adored their father. They would always say he was the 'fun one' and I was the 'boring one.' I am sure they were feeling neglected and sad based on the way their father was pulling away from them. They couldn't understand why and wondered if they did something to upset him. This was tough shit for little kids to deal with. I gave 200 percent to the kids to try to make up for what they were missing, but in my heart, I knew that what they were watching and experiencing would impact them for the rest of their lives, and it broke my heart."

"Why didn't you kick him out?"

"He was sick, and I knew it, so the compassionate part of me just hoped and prayed daily that he would see that he needed help and would get it and our family would be back to 'normal.' I knew in my heart that I couldn't live like this for long. I couldn't believe the thoughts of divorce were going through my head again, but they were. I kept remembering the vows I had said in 1987 before my family, friends, and God. I had to try.

"In November, we headed to Newport, Rhode Island, for our sixteenth wedding anniversary. I knew he was seriously depressed during this trip, and I knew we were in deep trouble."

"Why was it so clear?"

"He would've rather have spent time in the room sleeping than hanging out shopping or walking. The other surefire reason was that he didn't want hotel sex. I'm sorry, and this is really a sexist comment, but every guy looks forward to going away and having hotel sex. They're built that way. I didn't know how much more patient I could be.

"At this point, I didn't know what else I could do. He wasn't going for help...and our kids were being impacted negatively. What was I supposed to do? No one could help me make the right choice. I was trying to figure it out, and man, was I struggling.

"We created separate lives. He gave me money for groceries, but he kept the rest of the money in his own account. I thought if he managed his own money, it would help with his self-confidence. I did notice a few lies, which was weird because I always believed him, and he really had no reason to lie. For example, he said he was giving money to a few of his friends he said needed it. I was not sure he was really doing that, but I also had to trust him. I did trust him, so I was not drilling him for additional information."

"And any intimacy?"

"No. It had been years. I was still sleeping alone. Every night, I went to bed alone. Many nights, I would cry myself to sleep. I never felt so alone in a house full of people. You know?"

"At this time, does your family know what's going on?"

"If they do, they haven't said anything. I have told a few girlfriends that I'm having some issues, but I haven't told my family. There was always a concern that my parents would view me as a failure. Remember, that's how I felt the first time around when things were not well in the relationship. I didn't want people to think that I couldn't make my marriage work and that I was ruining my daughters' lives. Part of me was very concerned that they wouldn't understand the hell I had lived all these years or support me."

"You really thought your parents would react negatively?"

"I had convinced myself of this, and it didn't allow me to move in a different direction.

"By December, it was evident that Kevin was totally disengaged from our family and I was becoming the one responsible for every action and every decision. I was overcompensating for what he wasn't doing. It was exhausting."

"Give me an example of the lack of responsibility."

"OK. Here's an example. It was December 2. I asked Kevin to take Courtney to hockey practice when I took Chloe to gymnastics. When Chloe and I arrived home from practice that evening, all the lights were on in the house and the outside lights were on also. When I asked why he didn't take her, his answer was that she didn't want to go and he didn't feel like making her.

"I was so flipping pissed that he was so lazy that he would allow her to choose whether to go or not. That's not how you raise a child. We were the parents; we made the rules, and we taught by our actions. Being a parent meant doing things the kids don't always like. Too bad! They didn't have to like us. They had to respect us as parents. Our parenting skills were so different. I couldn't fight him on how to raise the girls. He really needed to understand how important it was to lead by example and teach the kids that when you commit to something, like hockey, that you stick to it even on the days you don't want to!

"Christmas was coming, and we needed to get through it as happily as possible for the family. Every Christmas Eve, I had my own little tradition. I put the kids to bed, and after I put out the stockings and presents and ate the Santa cookies, I'd grab a blanket, one glass of white wine, and my box of Kleenex and watch *It's a Wonderful Life*. I always cry at the ending. Having friends and family that stand by you in the darkest hour is truly the best gift a person can have. This Christmas Eve, I said a little prayer, 'Please, God, *please* let 2004 be a happy and healthy year!'"

Chapter 6

Advice to Others

"You've shared a lot about what your life has been like up to this point. I'd like to take a break and open it up for some questions from the audience at this time."

"Sure, I would be happy to answer any questions."

"First question comes from the young lady with auburn hair in the blue shirt second row."

"Thanks. My question is do you wish you did something differently, and if so, what would it be?"

"That's a tough question to answer. My first response would be that I should have called off the wedding at the first signs of trouble. I should have left. However, I didn't. If that had happened, I never would have had my daughters or become the woman I am today. Everything we do makes us stronger, and we become the people we are. Life is a journey, building blocks of events that make us better people. If you change one thing, who's to say the rest of your life would remain the same? Did I answer your question?"

"Yes, thank you. It just seems like you went through so much pain and you stuck it out to try to make it work."

"Yes, you are absolutely right. Who knows what my life would have been had I not gotten married or perhaps delayed it for five years until we knew each other more."

Sarah turned back to the audience. "Let's take our next question. Let's go to the gentleman over on the right about ten rows back. Black jeans, green shirt with yellow stripes, and tan baseball cap."

The gentleman stood up and asked, "What advice would you give to men?"

"Always treat your ladies with respect. No excuses. A relationship is a two-way street, and that fifty-fifty stuff is bullshit. In order to make it work, each person needs to give 100 percent. If both partners give 100 percent, there's a good chance that the partnership will work. The other thing that I would strongly urge is that if or when you see other men who are veering down the wrong path, say something. I wonder if someone had given feedback or guidance to Kevin earlier in his life, perhaps he would not have had to experience all the challenges he faced."

"Last question before we take a commercial break. Let's go to the woman all the way in the back. Pink shirt, white skirt, blond hair pulled back in a barrette. Yes, you, please."

"I'm in a relationship where my boyfriend is very controlling. He doesn't like me to see my girlfriends, and he's always checking my voice messages and e-mails to see where I've been and what I'm doing. I also think he has a drinking problem. He can't seem to stop at one or two drinks. What should I do?"

"I'm going to guess that you love him and that's why you are still with him. Is this correct?"

"Yes."

"If you feel bad about yourself or feel you have to behave in a manner that you don't like when you are with him, it is not a healthy relationship and you should end it. If he's drinking every day and can't stop, it's a sign of trouble ahead. Any healthy relationship would encourage you to spend time with your girlfriends. Love is not jealous, and relationships need to have separate interests so that when you spend time together, you have lots to talk about."

"But I don't want to be alone."

"May I ask how old you are?"

"I'm seventeen."

"You will never be alone in your life when you have the love of your family and friends. Settling for less in a relationship is not what you deserve. Respect yourself, stand up, and say you deserve more. Believe that you deserve more. Love will find its way to you. Love yourself first, and open your heart. It will come. I wasn't much older than you when I met and started dating Kevin. You're braver than me and wiser. You see the signs. You are asking the right questions about the potential issues. You need to make decisions not to be part of a negative relationship and to walk away while you easily can."

Sarah turned to the audience and said, "Thank you all for your engagement in the discussion and sharing your personal experiences and questions. We need to take a short commercial break. We will be back in ten minutes."

"Stephanie, I kept thinking to myself during break that if I was in your situation, I would've left him so much earlier."

"I would have thought that of myself also. But I couldn't walk. Think about all the thousands of women who are in a verbally or physically abusive relationship and they stay. There's something about staying. I'm not the first person who stayed in an abusive relationship, and I will not be the last. I think we're trained as very young children to learn to be loyal, to stick through the bad times, even if the bad times are really bad.

"When I got married, it was truly for better or for worse. I believe you make that commitment, and together you make it work. Communication and trust are the key factors that keep a relationship on a level that's open and honest. Married couples are partners, working towards a common goal. If one hurts, they share and together the team figures out how they will make things right. Our relationship was not like this. Over the years, I tried and wasn't ready to accept it would not be."

"It's time to return from commercial break and return to the discussion around the day that your life changed - *again.*"

Slowly, I took a deep breath, gently pushed the bangs away from my eyes and placed the hair behind my right ear, and readied myself for the reason for coming on the show.

Chapter 7

The Day Our Lives Changed Forever

" Chloe and I had started taking an exercise class at a local church in the fall of 2003. New Year's Day is always low key to us—time to chill before we go back to work after the holidays. When we returned from class on that January 1, 2004, day, we pulled into the driveway as we had done so many times before. I drove the car into the garage, grabbed our stuff out of the trunk, closed the garage door, and entered the house through the basement. At first, I didn't realize Kevin was in the cellar, but then as I began to walk up the stairs, I heard a noise in the corner of the room. I turned around and stepped back down the stairs to ask him what he was doing. He slowly turned toward me with tears in his eyes and said, "I need to tell you something but not right now." He turned to the wall with his shoulders shaking. I could see that he had started to cry.

"I stood quietly for a minute to register what he had just said, and then I heard myself say, '*What?* You can't throw out a statement like that and then decide not to discuss it. I don't think so. That's not fair.' I'd been waiting for months, almost a year, to find out what was going on, and finally, it appeared he was ready to talk. He needed to start talking. At first, I wasn't sure if I had this conversation out loud or if I was thinking it. When my eyes met Kevin's, I knew I had spoken the words out loud. He was digesting my comments. I just stared blankly at him as I waited for a response. As I waited, I sent Chloe upstairs.

Whatever was about to be discussed was not for our small daughter to listen to.

"In the seconds, which felt like minutes, my thoughts began to spin through my mind. I thought it was an affair—based on his distance, lack of interest in sex, and his late and random hours. I had prepared myself to hear the word *affair* come out of his mouth. All other reasons went in and out of my mind quickly. There was no other reason for his behavior, I believed. I slowly stepped backward to steady myself against the cellar wall. The words that came out of his mouth blew my world apart."

"I can't imagine. Well, I can imagine all kinds of stuff. What did he say?" Sarah asked.

Kevin said, 'I spent *all* the money in my bank account and our joint bank account.'

"I looked at him and said, 'What? You *fucking* did what? For the last year or so, you said you were putting all of the money from your check other than what you give me for groceries in your bank account so that we could go on a nice trip or you could buy your dream bass boat!' I took a few short gasps of air in, and then at the top of my lungs, I screamed, 'You did *what*? How much?' Louder and out of control, I repeated with my hands in fists and my teeth clamped down. '*How much?*'

"More than thirty thousand," Kevin timidly whispered.

"I couldn't believe this was happening. The room was spinning. I couldn't breathe. I felt like I was suffocating and the ceiling was falling down. I slowly walked along the wall, using the wall as my support. One step, two steps, three steps, and then I slowly sat on the bottom step of the cellar stairs and heard myself saying over and over, 'This is not happening. This is not happening. This is not happening.'

I had to put my head between my knees as the bile backed up into my throat. I couldn't believe this was occurring. I rocked back and forth, and inside my head, I heard my voice say, '*Breathe; breathe, breathe.*' I choked back the vomit that was rising in my throat. I could feel the salty tears rolling down my nose and rolling into the corner of my mouth.

"It was probably only five minutes before the room stopped spinning, but it felt more like thirty. I took a deep breath and said inside my head, *OK, you need to pull yourself together. Kevin did what he did, and you can't change it. Figure out what to do.* I took a deep and shaky breath and stopped crying.

"So, I calmly turned toward him and said to him, 'Exactly how/why/for what did you spend all the money?'

"'It was gambling,' Kevin quietly whispered with tears rolling down his face.

"'Gambling? Are you f'n' kidding me? Show me the bank account. I don't believe you!' I screamed at him.

"He reached up over his head, pushed up the pitted white ceiling panel, reached in, and pulled out the bankbooks from their hiding place. I didn't even know he had a hiding place. Sure as shit, he handed me the books for me to see with my own eyes that the balance was zero. I was floored. I could not comprehend how all of that money was gone. Why didn't I see the signs? How much I trusted him! How stupid I felt. Very, very stupid. *I'm an idiot.*

"I exhaled, sat there for a minute, and then started firing off more questions in rapid succession without a breath between each one: How long has this been going on? What type of gambling? Are we at risk to lose the house? Do you still owe money? Is anyone going to come and hurt us? Why didn't you tell me when you were in for five or ten thousand dollars? ***Why did you wait until all the money was gone?*** What the hell is your problem? You're such an asshole!"

"Wow. You must've been livid." Sarah looked at me in disbelief.

"I was so angry! I was so hurt. I've never been as devastated in my life as I was at that time. My anger was beyond comprehension. There were so many emotions running through me—anger, no hate! Sadness, disappointment, fear, and shame. We worked hard to build this account, to have financial security. I couldn't even begin to understand how someone could be so selfish to impact his family so negatively. It was surreal. This was the first time I'd felt that I was living outside of my body. This was not my life. This was not happening to me. Through pounding tears, inside, I cried, *Wake up! Wake up!*"

"But it wasn't a dream, was it? You didn't wake up, did you?"

"No. I never awoke. It wasn't a dream. I sobbed on and off for the rest of the day. All he did was apologize again and again. I couldn't understand. I would leave the room and then return to ask questions to try to understand. I couldn't comprehend. I was in shock. It was incomprehensible.

"I went upstairs to see the girls huddled on the couch together in silence. The girls didn't know what to do. They knew something bad was happening, but all I could say was, 'Daddy spent a lot of money without talking to Mommy. Mommy is very upset.'

"Before bed that night, I walked downstairs after the girls were in bed. I stood in front of him as he lay on the couch and said five simple words. There were no tears, no yelling, just, "Get help, or get out.

"Shortly after those words, I continued to explain that I couldn't do this anymore. 'I stood by you ten years ago, and I can't do it again and deal with another ten-year cycle. You have thirty days to begin to fix yourself, or you can pack your bags and get out. The girls and I love you very much, but we will not be put second place to anything. We deserve the best in life, and I won't put them at risk. I can't. I won't. I just won't."

"You had enough?"

"Everyone has a point when it's over. This was my tipping point. My second *poof.*

"The next morning, Kevin said he owed over five thousand to someone for gambling debts and he had to pay them a little each week. I wanted so hard to believe him; I wanted not to be deceived any longer. I wanted to trust what he was saying, but I just didn't. His admission made sense to some of our previous conversations around why he was saying he was giving money to friends who needed it over the past few months. Turned out it wasn't to help. It was for gambling debts. Once trust and faith are shattered, what's left to a relationship? I went to bed alone again and cried. I prayed for strength to get through life's latest challenge. My decisions would not only impact me but my girls. I had to make sure I was making the right choices for all of us. I looked for guidance.

"It was like being hit by a truck from behind. Never saw it coming. You know what I mean? I was devastated."

"How were the next thirty days?"

"The next month was very quiet in our house. Kevin went to work five of the next twenty days and laid on the couch the rest of the time.

"I had given him the month to show me in actions that he was going to face his battle straight-on and get counseling. Any sign for me to believe he cared. He did nothing, *nothing!* For the first time in our relationship, I was no longer going to be the enabler. I was done. I made a promise to myself ten years earlier that if he ever did something again that was verbally, physically, or emotionally putting his daughters or me at risk, I would walk away. No matter how hard it was going to be, I was keeping that promise to myself. It was so hard to just go through the motions every day and not ask if he made an appointment to get some help. I knew I could no longer help him. Whatever he chose to do was his decision. So on the thirty-first day, I filed for divorce. I knew I was affecting three lives irreparably. I didn't take that lightly.

"Through this experience, I knew I could never control someone else's actions. I could only control my own. That realization would remain with me forever and became a guiding principal as I faced other life challenges. *Control what you can control. Let the rest go.*

"Telling my family was the second most difficult thing I had to do; telling my girls was the first. I tried multiple times to call my parents and tell them. The words would form on my lips but never pass through to the air to be heard by others. I couldn't get them out. When I finally realized I couldn't, I wrote a letter and gave it to my sister on a simple Saturday morning when I was dropping off Chloe for a fun day with her favorite aunt and uncle. I asked her to read it later that day and then to pass it along to Mom and Dad and ask them to pass it along to our brother. Although I knew in my head that it was not my fault that we were going to get a divorce, I still had too much embarrassment to actually have the words, 'I'm getting divorced' pass through my lips.

"That weekend, Kevin and I planned to sit the girls down at the kitchen table to tell them that we were getting divorced. I felt strongly that Kevin should explain it to them since many of his choices led us down the path and it was the reason why we were in these shoes."

"Did you take any responsibility for the divorce?"

"I understand that it takes two to make or break a relationship so I know I owned responsibility, but at the time, I didn't feel like it was a fifty-fifty responsibility. I hadn't spent all the family's money and put my selfish needs in front of my family. Yes, I owned a little; he owned a lot."

"So, you guys sat down together and told the girls?"

"We sort of sat down together. He said he wouldn't tell the girls. I was pissed. This was just another example of how irresponsible, immature, and selfish he was and just another confirmation that I was doing the right thing. I told him he had to at least sit there and answer questions. Of course, I had to deliver the message. I wasn't surprised, but I was disappointed that he couldn't man-up.

"We sat down on a Saturday afternoon. There we were. The worst thing in a child's life is the realization that their parents would not be together. Their life would be shattered, I knew. I would need to be strong and do everything I could to minimize the most painful discussion the girls would have in their very young lives. I gathered up the girls, who were each hanging out in their individual bedrooms. Courtney was on her computer and Chloe in her room lying across her bed reading a book. We all walked to the kitchen and settled at the table. Kevin was already sitting there sobbing as we walked up to him. With the warm sun flowing into the window and the scent of flowers in the room, it would have been a perfectly beautiful day, but it wasn't going to be anything close to perfect or beautiful. Chloe had the fear of God in her eyes, and Courtney, well, I think she already knew why we were there. So, in my bravest, strongest voice, I began, 'Your father and I have decided to get divorced.'

"Before the word *divorce* rolled off my tongue, Courtney said, 'I knew it!' and she got up, slammed her fist on the tabletop, and stormed out of the room.

"Chloe screamed at the top of her lungs, 'No! No! No!'

"Their actions pierced through my heart like an ice-cold blade. All of your life, as a parent, you try to protect your children. You make choices to help them grow, to be strong, to be happy. The pain in their voices was unequivocally devastating. Courtney's actions broke my heart. We had just pulled a rug out from under them. In thirty seconds, we had changed their lives forever. Everything they believed in, everything that made them secure, family unity—it was gone. The innocence of childhood was shattered. Would they ever forgive me?

"I sat for a moment, turned to Kevin, and gave him the most evil, penetrating look from across the table. I stood up and found each of the girls, put my arms around them, and walked them back to the table. As we all sat back down, in a low whisper, I said, 'We will be OK.' Even as I heard the words dangle in the air, I didn't know how we would make it through. I told them in my reassuring, confident voice, 'Mommy has a good job. We will be OK. Daddy will be finding an apartment, and we will help him buy furniture and help him move. We will continue to see him, and he loves you both very much. We just cannot live together any longer.'"

"Did Kevin say anything?"

"Not a word. He sat with his head in this hands and tears rolling down his face. He didn't even look up at the girls.

"I did not tell them that Kevin had a gambling problem during this family meeting. That would come much later. They had enough to digest.

"The day I decided to file, I made a conscious decision to take the high road through the whole ugly divorce process that I knew I was going to face. I knew that most people would understand my choices. Some wouldn't agree and would feel I should be sticking it out in the marriage, and I knew they would challenge my convictions. I would never speak negatively about Kevin to the girls. He was their father, and I would be as respectful as possible, regardless of what he did to himself or to us.

"I was being my logical self. I wasn't prepared for the overwhelming feeling of failure. I succeeded in my job. I succeeded in raising my family. I succeeded in sports or games. I was a winner. But in my marriage, I lost. I was a loser. I couldn't make it work. I had failed. It was really tough for me. It was very difficult to realize I was a failure."

"How long did you guys have to live together before Kevin moved out?"

"It was about a month after I filed, so about sixty days since I found out what was going on. I had to find him an apartment and buy the furniture, put down the security deposit, and pay the first month's rent. He couldn't find the steps to move forward. I even made curtains for his windows. He was not capable of getting organized to move on any of this. Unfortunately, if I left it to him, I think we would still be living in the same house.

"The day Kevin moved out was a family affair. I felt strongly that it was important for the girls to know where Kevin was going to live and to handle the move as positively as possible. Both the girls, myself, and my parents moved his stuff in and cleaned his apartment, and then we left and the girls and I returned to our beautiful two-thousand-plus-square-foot colonial. We left Kevin in his two-room apartment. Although I felt bad, I knew that this was the consequence for the choices he made. There were no other options.

"I cried myself to sleep as I had for so many days in the past and as I would for many nights over the next six months. I cried more in those six months than all the years before and all the years since. I was scared. I didn't know if I could do this. I didn't know if he owed bad people money and they would try to hurt the girls and me. I kept a strong front to the girls, but inside, I was very, very fearful. I moved all the remaining money to the girls' names and talked to the lawyer about putting a lien on our home so that if he did owe anyone anything, they could not touch the house. The lawyer did that immediately, and I was able to breathe a little bit easier. It was probably a year before I didn't fear coming home to the house and didn't fear the cars that drove down the cul-de-sac and slowed but never stopped and that those phone calls where there was a caller but no message left were from Kevin's gambling debts. The loss of security and the entrance of that fear really made me angry at Kevin.

"The morning after Kevin moved out, before I got out of bed, I wrote the following list of promises to myself on the notepad on my side table. A few days later, I typed it up and taped it to the wall on the right side of my east-facing bedroom window. Nothing fancy, just a plain white piece of paper that listed words. Each morning, when I got out of bed to start my day, I would read these promises I made to myself. I would put the smile on my face because I was in charge of my life and the lives of my girls and whatever the day was going to bring—I knew I could take it on. I had to take it on. I was going to take it on. I had a choice to focus on all the negatives (and there were a lot!) or focus on the positives. I chose the latter. Can you project the list of the screen? I would like to read each of the items to our audience."

> I promise to begin each day happy.
> I will remember all the joy (past, present, and future) in my life.
> I will be thankful for the gifts I have been given.
> I will not dwell on my challenges or sadness.
> I will be thankful for:
> - my wonderful girls
> - my family
> - my friends
> - the miracle of the sunrise and the beauty of a sunset
> - the rebirth of springtime
> - good health
> - laughter and love

I will not feel sorry for myself.
I will remember I am never alone.
I am wonderful and know that someday I will find love again.
I will choose to look at the positive in every situation.
I will never regret my decision—never.
There is nothing I cannot handle.

"You read that every morning?"

"Every single morning for about a year when I got out of bed and watched the sun begin to rise over the horizon outside of my bedroom window. I found strength in those words, and I had to believe in them. Some days, those words and the power of the sunrise were the only things that kept me moving forward."

"I heard that you find strength in reading quotes."

"Yes, I do. Here's one that I read often as I felt it was very fitting at this time in my life: 'Keep your fears to yourself, but share your courage with others' by Robert Louis Stevenson."

Chapter 8

The Washing Machine Lesson

"Things continued to progress for the final divorce proceedings. In April 2004, I had completed the parenting class at the local clinic as required by state law. Three weeks later, I ran into one of the guys from the class at the grocery store. At first, I didn't remember how I knew him. He approached me in the frozen-food aisle and asked how my divorce was going. When I looked at him questioningly, he reminded me that we were in the divorce class together. I immediately began to wonder what went wrong in his relationship and what he did to cause his marriage to fall apart. I stood there and began to judge him. I felt horrible. What a bitch I was. I knew that there would be many people who would do the exact same thing to me—wonder what I did to make my marriage fall apart, what *I* did wrong, what *I* should have done differently to keep my marriage together. After grabbing for an ice cream, I excused myself and wished him the best as his divorce became final. He asked me to meet him for dinner sometime. I politely declined. I wasn't ready. Plus, I couldn't remember his name. Would I ever be ready again to risk my heart with someone else? I wondered if anyone would ever love me for who I was and want all that I could give. I still can't believe I didn't know what was going on in my own life. How could I ever trust completely again? How was I so blind?

"There was no way I was going to get involved with anyone in 2004. I made that promise to myself. This was a year of adjustment for the girls and me. I was not going to introduce anyone into our lives. I knew it would take at least a year or so before things could become 'normal' for us—whatever the new 'normal' would be. I also knew that the girls needed to get used to the idea that their father was no longer going to be in their lives on a daily basis and introducing anyone new into their lives would not be fair. I had to think of them and their needs in front of mine."

"Was that hard? To commit to not dating for a year?"

"No, not really. When I made the decision to get divorced, I knew it would turn the girls' lives upside down, and I promised myself to support their needs in this transition period first and my needs second. I never believed that you needed a man to be happy. You have to be happy with yourself, by yourself, and then if love comes, it's just icing on the cake."

"So, it was the 'girls against the world'?"

"Yes, and we were managing OK. One afternoon, we had a little show-and-tell on where the circuit box was in the garage, how to reset a circuit, how to shut the water off in the back of a toilet (if it doesn't stop running), how to unclog a toilet, and how to stop the water filling the washing machine, the phone numbers of the neighbors, and we ran through the emergency procedures if there was a fire in the house—where we would meet, how we would exit the house if various exits were blocked due to fire or smoke. I figured there were some things the girls needed to be prepared for in case a little emergency came up whether I was at home or not.

"We settled into our normal new schedule. I drove the girls to school in the morning, they arrived home via the bus, or I picked them up after school when their activities were done, and then we had dinner together, watched TV, did homework, and went to bed.

"A couple months later, our show-and-tell came in handy when we experienced our first little house disaster. It was a Sunday, and I was doing laundry (as I always do, once a week on the weekends). I was watching TV, and Courtney was on the computer in the other room. Next thing I hear is Courtney tearing around the corner through the kitchen and down the hall to the downstairs bathroom. She shut off the washing machine water and popped into the living room to exclaim that the rug in the computer room was soaked. I went into the bathroom and found just a slight bit of water on the floor, so, I instructed the girls to head upstairs and grab some bath towels. Chloe and I started sopping up the water in the family room carpet, and Courtney headed into the basement. When she ran back up the stairs, she stared at me and firmly stated that I *did not* want to go downstairs and look in the garage. Of course, I moved quickly downstairs and threw open the cellar door to see buckets of water pouring through the ceiling of the garage, through the garage door openers, through the light fixtures, and onto the car. It was raining in my garage. I took a deep breath and walked upstairs. Courtney took one look at me and said, 'You going to start to cry?'

"I said, 'No, not right now.' Then we stood there in the kitchen right next to the kitchen table, and all three of us looked at each other bewildered about what to do. We asked out loud what would daddy do? And we giggled a little and said, 'He'd call Papa.' Then we gave each other a little hug and grabbed the phone. Mom answered, and I asked her to have Papa grab his tools and swing over to the house. The washing machine tub had a leak and we had water everywhere. I needed help."

"You needed help. Bet those were tough words to say out loud."

"Yes. I needed help. Hmmm. Three simple but very powerful words. Those three words were very difficult to say for many years after the divorce. I was independent and strong; I didn't want to need help. It was only years later that I realized asking for help was OK and didn't mean I was a failure or weak. The failure was when I knew I needed help but was too proud to ask for it. This Sunday afternoon, I was no longer too proud. I became smart. I called in the cavalry.

"Shortly thereafter, my dad was pulling into the driveway in the tan Buick. Mom was driving. I was surprised to see them both, but Mom came over for moral support...I went next door to see if my neighbors, Nick and Linda were home. Linda and I had become good friends over the years since they had moved it. We spent time together in the garden talking about our lives or sharing our gardening experiences. She and I both found solitude pulling weeds and nurturing our perennial gardens. I knew if Nick was home, he would be willing to come over and help. I strolled the 500 feet to the tan split level ranch to the right of our home. As I had expected, Nick came over quickly and together, he and my dad took care of sucking up all the water in both the tub of the washer and in the rug with the shop vac. Linda came over to see if I needed help as Dad and Nick pulled the washer out of the tight space in the half bathroom closet, down the hall, and out the front door. After we cleaned up as much as we could, Mom, Dad, Linda, and Nick headed back to their homes. The girls and I cleaned up everything else, and Courtney turned to me and said, 'You going to cry now?'

"My response was, 'Yup.' The tears began to pour down my face. We all laughed, and she handed me a tissue. It lasted only a few minutes, and those tears symbolized both sadness in having to do this by myself and pride in my ability to get it done—even if getting it done meant asking for help. Keeping the house after the divorce provided some stability to the girls, and I was going to make it work, no matter what. I knew keeping up the house would be a challenge. Asking for help was no longer a challenge. From that incident forward, I was able to get support whenever needed."

"On that Sunday afternoon, you survived your first house disaster and you all learned an important lesson that day. What do you think the girls took away as a lesson?"

"They may not recognize it until they are older and wiser, but in the duration of a sunny Sunday afternoon, they learned that: We are independent, strong females who will get through whatever we are faced with. Relying on our friends and family is not an indication of weakness; it's being able to recognize when help is needed and having the courage and strength to reach out. People who love you will always help, and we sometimes need to swallow our pride and ask."

Chapter 9

Vacationing Alone

❝The summer came with another milestone. It was the first family vacation to Maine that the girls and I would go on alone. This was one of many family traditions that would be continued and altered at the same time. I knew traditions would keep the girls grounded during the divorce, so we went ahead with this vacation. Kevin volunteered to house and dog sit for us while we were gone.❞

"Wait! You guys have been separated for about six months now. You let him back into your home?"

"Yes. However, it was not without some hesitation. Part of me felt it wasn't a good idea, but he was in a studio apartment and I felt that it might be a good thing for him to spend some time in a larger space. I hesitated at his suggestion and prayed he would be strong enough to stay in a home he no longer owned (he quit-claimed the house over to me in the spring). As we pulled away from the house, Kevin was in the truck, ready to pull into the driveway. I could feel my eyes well up as I fought back the tears. 'Have a great trip!' he gently called as we drove away slowly. Courtney asked me why my eye was watering. I told a fib and told her I had an eyelash in my eye. I knew full well the real reason was that I was leaving for a vacation without the man I had been building a life with for the last sixteen years. I'm sure she probably knew it was well, but we both sat silently as I made the sign of the cross and said the 'Our Father' under my breath as my father had done on the trips as youngsters, praying silently for a safe trip.

"Three hours later, we arrived in Maine. The weather was overcast, wet, and dreary, but that was not going to dampen our spirits. We were off to spend five glorious days on the Maine seacoast away from work and all of the other concerns and troubles in our lives. The house we rented was a four-bedroom white clapboard colonial with kelly-green shutters and flower boxes adorning each window with geraniums, alyssums, marigolds, and impatiens. The house was perched high above Short Sands Beach in York, and the wrap-around porch provided great views of the ocean, overlooking a hill of sea roses and a buoy in the harbor that rang with every ebb and flow of the ocean tide.

"The green wicker rockers and hammock swayed in the ocean breeze. After we unpacked the car, we relaxed and enjoyed each other's company on the back deck with our iced tea and chocolate-chip cookies. It's amazing how the sounds and smells of the ocean help to put life into perspective.

"During the week, we walked the beaches, shopped in the quaint shops of Ogunquit, watched taffy being made at the Goldenrod, bowled at the oceanfront alley, and strolled along Marginal Way. It was a great week.

"On Saturday, we packed up the car and returned home. Both the house and the dog were still intact when we arrived. Nothing seemed to be missing, and I hated the fact that I had to worry that someone I had spent years with could actually do harm to us or the home we built together. But unfortunately, he wasn't the same person I married many years ago.

"As these thoughts ran through my mind, I went upstairs to put my clothes and makeup away. I opened the toilet to go pee, and there was a mouse doing the dead-man's float in the bowl."

"A dead mouse in the toilet?"

"Yes. Very strange, I thought. We never had a mouse problem or even a single mouse in the house. I pulled the floater out of the bowl, placed him in a plastic bag, and threw him out and then ran to the store to pick up some traps. The traps we laid all over the house never met the fate of a mouse."

"What do you think happened with that mouse?"

"To this day, I still believe it was Kevin who put that mouse into its floating pool. He denied it, but I do not believe him. I kept thinking that instead of a dead horse's head in my bed, it was a floating mouse in my toilet. It was way too coincidental. Maybe it wasn't him. We'll never know."

"That is a weird coincidence. Ever see a mouse in the house after that incident?"

"Nope. Never saw a mouse again. Maybe nothing, but to this day, I still think it's very questionable."

Chapter 10

Countdown

"So, after six months, you're at the countdown week to the divorce. That week must have been very stressful."

"Yes. Some days just stick in your memory forever. This one I won't forget. July 16, 2004 – five days to D-Day (Divorce – Day). The week started off on the wrong foot. Bright and early Monday morning, I got a call from my lawyer who said the court appearance might get postponed since Kevin didn't do the required parenting class. I was so pissed! This was so typical of our relationship. He couldn't even do one simple thing, which was required and would provide some closure for our girls and me. Ugh!

"That evening, Kevin called to see if I would give him his ten thousand dollars cash in advance of the divorce so that he could go and buy a boat this weekend. My first thought was, *Screw you! I may not even be able to take the final step to get divorced because you're a stupid ass…and you want me to give you cash up front? Hell no!* Even my lawyer said no to the cash advance. Things seemed very questionable; something was wacky. Why couldn't he wait *five* days? So, I didn't give it to him. I ended up paying Kevin's car taxes and registration on the truck that month, and I wasn't giving him one more cent. It was horrible that he spent all the money in his bank account and all the money in our joint account. I had to spend the money I had saved in my own account on the divorce and all the other expenses. I wasn't giving him a freakin' cent until I absolutely had to.

"Four days to D-Day, July 17, 2004, as I cooked up the kids' eggs and bacon for breakfast, I could hear the truck pull into the driveway. I turned down the stove, took a breath in, and walked to the back deck to see Kevin stepping out of his truck. He had stopped over to wash his truck."

"What? You let him come over to wash his truck?"

"Yes, I did. He asked if he could come over, and I said yes. I was trying very hard to continue to be nice to him for the sake of the girls. I allowed him to come over to the house for two reasons. It was cheaper to use my water and the central vacuum system than it was to go to the carwash, and it would allow the girls to see him without them making plans with him and having him cancel at the last moment, breaking their hearts.

"As he got out of his truck, you could see the sadness surround him as his shoulders sank low. Normally, I would feel a little tinge of pity for him but not today. Today, I was angry. I am not sure I woke up angry, but as I fried the bacon and eggs, I grew angrier knowing that he was coming over. I was angrier because he chose to do drugs and spend thousands of dollars that should have been for us. *Oh* yes, I forgot to mention, I found out it was drugs and not gambling at all."

"What, drugs? That's a little worse than gambling."

"You think? I'll tell you how I found out in a few minutes.

"There were other angry thoughts brewing as I waited for him to hook up the hose. I was angry that my life was turned upside down. I was angry because he could come and go; he had no responsibility weighing on his shoulders. He would scoot through life without the guilt and pressure of making the right or wrong decision for every choice that needed to be made for the girls—*our* girls. I stood there for a few minutes, and all of these painful and hurtful thoughts started to flood into my head. All I could think was, ***I'm going to be alone for the rest of my life.*** I started to feel the tears well in my eyes. I fluttered my eyelids as hard as I could. I was not going to give him the satisfaction of seeing the hurt he had caused. Once again. I wasn't going to cry in front of him. I wouldn't. I choked back the tears, walked down the stairs of the deck, and marched right up to him. I got in his face and began to speak. It sounded something like this: 'Take the damn parenting class. I don't want to have the divorce date moved. I need closure. I need to move on.' I begged him, pleaded for him to do this one thing for me, one simple thing, with tears streaming down my face. He promised he would.

"I knew he was lying, like he had lied to me so many times before. I chose to believe him, just for this moment, because I couldn't accept not to. I asked him how he was doing, and as usual, his answer was 'fine.' *Fine?* No one is fine when his life is falling apart. We stood there, in the driveway, for a few moments, and then as tears began to roll down his face, he said five words that expressed exactly how he felt: 'My life ends this week.'

"I stood there quietly. I didn't say a word. I waited, and he continued with the following: 'Don't ever think it was your fault. This had nothing to do with you. You are wonderful and beautiful, and someday you will find that someone who can give you everything you deserve. This whole mess has been my fault.'

"I knew it, and he knew it. I'd waited for months to hear him accept what he did. I thought hearing the words from him would make things a little better, but it didn't. I just made me sad and worried for him, sorry that he chose the coward's way out and didn't have the courage to face his demons and get help, sorry that he destroyed our family. I felt sorry for him. I would survive and knew in my heart (not always my head) that one day I would be loved and with my girls, I would always be blessed. I was not sure he would. I knew that the only one who could help Kevin was Kevin. He needed to hit rock bottom to begin the crawl back up. I didn't think he had hit rock bottom yet."

"How and when did you find out that Kevin didn't have a gambling problem?"

"I don't remember the exact date. But after Kevin moved out, he told me he was doing cocaine and heroin. He did explain that it started with prescription painkillers (Oxycontin) for the back injury and then went from one drug to another, chasing the high.

"That was surprising to me but not shocking. What was more upsetting was when I found out that my father knew that he had been doing Oxy in the summer of 2003 and hadn't told me. I was blown away. Everything about that summer vacation and Kevin's behavior now made perfect sense. I understood why he was so anxious - he was high all the time.

"At first, I couldn't comprehend why my father chose Kevin over me, just as I couldn't understand why Kevin chose drugs over me. Was I really that unimportant to others that I could be the bottom of the priority chain? It was only months later that I accepted my father's logic in that he'd made a promise to Kevin. It was very difficult for me to accept that the girls and I were at risk for many months with Kevin's irrational behavior and we never knew it until later.

"I was pissed because I didn't know if he was sharing needles, and although he said he wasn't, how could I believe him after all the lies? My worst fear was that his selfish stupidity would result in my getting HIV. My physical health was the immediate concern. Kids couldn't be without both their parents. So, off I went to the doctor to get the full blood work done to make sure I didn't have HIV."

"Did your results come back negative?"

"Yes. Then once I knew that I was OK, I could deal with my father."

"Do you still speak to your father?"

"Yes, of course. I love my Dad. I understand his logic for not say-ing anything to me based on his promise to Kevin, and it is an honor-able character to keep your word to someone but not under every circumstance. Sometimes you have to break a promise if someone more important to you could be hurt if you keep the secret. I think in this case, he should have seen the potential impact and harm to his daughter and granddaughters and broken the promise. He made the decision that was right for him. I get it. I don't agree with why he did it and it was pretty hard for me to accept; however, I eventually forgave him. Harboring anger wasn't something I had the energy for.

"July 21, 2004 was D-Day. The morning of the divorce was tough. It was the final stage. I still struggled with the feelings of failure and knew that this would be closure on a very large part of my life.

"First thing Kevin said to me in the morning was that he wanted the money I owed him immediately after the divorce was final. I knew it was to purchase drugs. Drugs right after the divorce was final, how screwed up! I was worried about taking care of our kids, and he was worried about how quickly and where he could score his next hit. Freakin' crazy! I wish I could say I was surprised, but I wasn't.

"So, we agreed to go to the bank after the proceedings were com-pleted. I had taken the day off of work, since I knew it would be a very emotional day.

"That afternoon when I got home, I wrote a letter to my staff and friends at work who supported me through the last seven months. It reflected all the emotions I felt on that day. Do you mind if I read it to you and the audience? Every time I read it, all the emotions from the day come rushing back."

"Of course, please."

"Excuse me in advance if I get choked up."

"Don't worry. It's OK if you get emotional. I'll grab the box of Kleenex that we stuffed under your seat for you just in case."

"'Dear Friends,'" I began. "'I'm home and divorced (that sounds so strange to say or to write). Thank you for all your good wishes and support over the last seven months as I struggled through the decisions and emotions of this huge life event. Instead of giving you all updates tomorrow, I thought I'd drop you a note. This way, I can begin to move forward, and also, I won't be bawling my eyes out at work or on the phone. You know there's always a story. Nothing is ever simple. Here's my story of today (please don't share this note).

"'I awoke to a splitting headache this morning (wonder why?), did my normal routine, and dressed for court. I went simple casual—but no jeans—also, no 'corporate' look since I knew we were already facing a financial challenge with the asset division. I found my first two gray hairs when I was plucking my eyebrows. I had to laugh. How perfect!

"'Phone rang about seven forty-five. It was Kevin. He realized he had no good pants to wear and needed his suit brought over—so typical! I finished getting ready and headed to his apartment. Of course, there were two suits and one of the pairs of pants was not on the hanger. It was eight forty-five, and we had to be in court by nine ten. I jumped in the car and drove across town (back to my house), get the pants, and realize they need to be ironed—Murphy was with us. I called Kevin to tell him he was going to have to wear the tight pants (couldn't find the others) and I'd meet him at the courthouse. By that time, I was starting to panic; it was nine.

"'I drove to the courthouse. I got a little bit lost and then got found, parked in the garage, and met Kevin on the front step of the courthouse. I'd never been to court. I thought I was going to puke.

"'I took the stairs and headed to the third floor. My lawyer was already there; it was nine fifteen. We stepped into a room to review the plan. The attorney called it a conference room; it was no bigger than my bathroom. I called it an interrogation room. I was waiting for the bright light to beam directly into my face. It didn't; I was thankful. I tried to concentrate. I looked over at Kevin. This was all so sad. The tears began to flow.

"'We reviewed the case. The lawyer was very concerned on how the judge would rule. I started to pull out the tissue, so much for putting makeup on. Kevin sat quietly next to me, choking back the tears. The lawyer and Kevin had to visit a representative in family services, trying to be as proactive as possible regarding the anticipated questions from the judge. I waited in the hallway, pacing back and forth. I couldn't help but overhear the couple next to me fighting over every aspect of their divorce, her lawyer talking to his, arguing louder and louder. I was thankful that was not me arguing.

"'It was now nine fifty-five, and the judge and court support came out. I was on my fifth tissue. We headed into the courtroom. Looked like Court TV or Judge Judy's courtroom. I heard a laugh coming out of my mouth—not sure what I expected but realized this was serious. Guess I thought we'd just be sitting around a table talking. Not quite what I imagined, it was a real courtroom!

"'The judge came in, and we all rose. Now we waited to get our case called. Kevin was angry; family services said he might be ordered to pay child support although he and I agreed he would not pay the child support if I was able to keep the house. He would only have to support the college expenses. I tried to reassure him it would be OK and it wouldn't happen. If it did, we'd figure something out. Two cases called, I watched them. No emotion, no feelings, so matter of fact. We listened as they divided their lives—who got what to every detail of their lives. I thought, *How sad.* It was now ten twenty, and we were the third case called.

"'We got sworn in, and I sat at the table to the right with my lawyer. Kevin was on his own to the left. The judge already made a comment regarding the asset division. The bailiff was on my right. It all became so real. I hoped I could hold it together. All I could think was that I'd failed and everyone was watching me and the details of the breakup of my marriage were open to the public. Kleenex number eight.

"'Fifteen minutes of questioning me, I was prepared. I answered correctly. The tears were being choked back. The judge started to question Kevin. He held it together. A lecture occurred regarding taking the parenting class. I was so pissed that he didn't finish it and was thankful that the judge told him he would be in contempt of court if he didn't complete it within ten days. The judge then challenged Kevin regarding the separation agreement. He answered well—what we wanted to hear, what the judge wanted to hear. Damn him for not taking that parenting class!

"'Listening to all of this just caused the emotions to break through in a flood of hysteria. The tears were flowing hard. The bailiff left the room and returned with a box of Kleenex, which he placed on the table in front of me. I'd gone through all the tissues in my pocket. I thanked him.

"'The whole court got to hear about our issues, our financials, how we were dividing up our lives—I thought this was horrible. What did they think? Did they look at me and think what a bitch I was? I really didn't care. I was thinking, *You need to stay focused and keep it together.*

"'It was ten forty-five. The judge was satisfied we were both in agreement. He went through the formal words...and decreed us divorced. It's over...

"'Sixteen years completed in twenty-five minutes.

"'We left the courtroom, and I shared a few words with my lawyer. I couldn't talk. I would call him later this week or next week to do my will and other paperwork that I needed to complete to ensure the girls were well taken care of. He asked if I was OK, and I responded, 'No, I'll call you...'

"'Outside, Kevin and I had a few words to share. We will each grieve in our own ways—in our own time. We met at the bank and transferred funds to begin the process of executing our agreement. He couldn't get that money fast enough.

"'The majority of the work is mine to do, and I will complete all required paperwork over the next week or so.

"'Am I OK? I have to be—I have no choice. I have my friends, my family, and much support. It's weird since I *never* expected in my life to be divorced, but we don't always have control over things that happen to us; we have control over how we handle them...and I believe I chose the right path for how to handle this situation in my life. The choices have not been easy, but I know in my heart that there is a better life for my girls and me.

"'I'm getting off the computer now (twentieth Kleenex) and heading outside to garden—my healing place. I'll see you guys tomorrow.

Thanks for everything! (I'll be back online tonight for a while.) Love, Stephanie.'

"After dinner of my divorce day, my girlfriend Kellie popped over unexpectedly with a bunch of blue hydrangeas wrapped with a purple bow, a card, and a hug. She wanted me to know that I was in her thoughts all day and she knew the pain I was feeling since she had recently been divorced.

"We hugged on my front porch, and although she stayed just a few minutes that afternoon, her simple visit meant the world to me. After she left, I read the Hallmark greeting card, and its simple words spoke volumes: 'Stepping onto a brand-new path is difficult but not more difficult than remaining in a situation which is not nurturing to the whole woman.'

"That was a great card. Its message was so true. I knew in my heart that although many challenges might lie in front of me, I had made the right choice."

"What an emotional ride over the last seven months. You must have been exhausted."

"Yes, both physically and emotionally. I had lost over twenty pounds during the divorce months, and I needed to start taking better care of myself. I knew that. I had to begin to put all the pieces together.

"I like to call July 22, 2004, the first day of my new life. For any of you who have been through a divorce, you know how symbolic it feels to start that new life. I could breathe again.

"Life was now full of possibilities and full of fear. For the longest time, I would read *Family Circle* magazine every month. I enjoyed their 'Words to Live By' feature, which presented inspirational quotes. I kept these pages in a folder and would pull them out whenever I needed a little perspective or inspiration. One issue was especially touching for me, and I posted it on the mirror of my bedroom armoire to remind me that I had a choice every morning on how I would handle the day. There were some days that I could barely do anything that was listed here, and there were other days when I would accomplish many things. Either way, the daily reminder was simple: 'Life is about choices!'

"Can we throw up on the screen my reminders that life is a choice and that I chose to live?"

"Let's look behind us—there they are."

Slowly, the words began to scroll up from the bottom, in a black script font against a blue background. The silence slowly transitioned across the audience as line by line, the reminders flowed. By the time, all nine lines were displayed on the screen; you could have heard a pin drop.

I think the audience understands. **Choices**

> The best accessory is a smile—wear one often.
> Fill your to-do list with things that make you happy.
> Share your blessings when you're feeling blessed.
> Never miss an opportunity to tell someone you love them.
> If you want something out of your day, put something into it.
> Share your thoughts to uplift, not undermine.
> Never let a kind word go unsaid.
> Teach what you know; learn what you don't.
> Remember that some things are urgent and others are important; know the difference.

Chapter 11

Divorced

"I'm divorced now. Day one. Every morning, I open my eyes, throw off the covers, pop out of bed, open the windows, and read my sayings. I take deep breath and look toward the sky to thank God that I have been given another day. For the most part, the days are routine: get the kids to school, off to work, then to volunteering or cheerleading or homework, dinner, TV or games, and off to bed. I think the girls are adjusting well (as well as can be expected), and I think I'm doing OK. Thank God for my parents and my sister and brother, who have volunteered to help, and they are there when I need them."

"So, now you're divorced. I'm sure things are starting to settle. How are you doing?"

"After the divorce was final, I learned that Kevin was still doing drugs. I also found out that he had been doing drugs for over eighteen months. I felt so stupid. I still couldn't believe I didn't know. In retrospect, I could see a few things that were probably signs. For example, he was throwing up almost every morning, keeping the outside front door light on at night (paranoia), taking lots of sleeping pills at night to try to get off the day's high and sleep. I didn't hear from him much over the next few months. He took a leave from work, and he struggled with his depression; there were weeks, literally, when we didn't hear from him."

"No word at all for weeks?"

"No, we heard nothing. The first time there was an extended period of silence was immediately after the divorce when we didn't hear a word for two weeks. The girls and I tried and tried to reach him, but he would never pick up the phone. I found myself driving by his apartment to see if the curtains had moved at all—see if there was any life in there. I began to dream that he was dead and began to set up a plan to determine how I was going to tell the girls, explain their father's suicide or drug overdose to them. I was so angry that he would put us through this and he was so selfish that he couldn't even call and let his daughters know how he was. They were worried sick for him, and once again, he was unable to provide them the comfort they so desperately needed.

"During his darkest period, he spent two periods of time at the Institute of Living. I don't know how or why he landed there either time, I only heard that he was there when he sent a letter to the girls. During his stay, I learned that he had attempted to kill himself in the institute by pulling a mirror off the wall, shattering the glass into manageable segments, grabbing onto one, and slitting his wrists with it."

"Were you surprised?"

"Nothing surprised me anymore. I was scared and sad for him but not surprised. The girls never knew what happened. They had enough to deal with without worrying that their father might not be around. I didn't feel it was worth telling them as I had hoped their father would turn around his life and it would be a non-issue.

"The second time we didn't hear from him for a significant period of time happened in September of the same year. Prior to this episode, the last time I tried to call and he didn't pick up the phone, I was in a panic. This time, when we could not get a hold of him, my feelings were more along the lines of *'Here we go again!'* and *'Screw you!'* I knew it was the wrong attitude to have, but I was so angry—bad enough that I had to worry but messing with the girls and making them go through this whole disappointment again. That was where I drew the line.

"Instead of trying to reach him, chase him down, drive by again and again and again, hoping to see a shade or a curtain move just a little bit to indicate life was inside, I decided it wasn't my problem anymore. It couldn't be. He was a big boy and was on his own to take care of himself. I had all I could handle with the girls. I still had not said anything negative to the girls about their father. When this silence occurred again, I didn't even address it with the girls for a while. I hoped that if I delayed telling them, that he would get ahold of himself and contact us and I could avoid the whole incident. The girls would never be the wiser.

"It was about two in the afternoon on September 14, 2004, a few weeks after we heard from him last, when I saw the '584' number on my caller ID at work. I didn't remember his number, so when I picked it up, I was surprised to hear his voice on the other end of the phone. Actually, I was shocked. I asked him how he was and if he was OK. He said he would get better starting today; his medication was increased. 'I hope so,' I responded. He said he was sorry for being such a jerk and not being there for the girls. I told him I didn't need his apology; there was nothing he could do for me but he needed to apologize to the girls. He said he wanted to come over and see the girls at six that night. I agreed but decided not to tell the girls because they didn't need to be disappointed (again!). I said I would see him later and hung up the phone, but I could hear the little voice in my head say, '*Sure you will. Don't say anything to the girls in case he doesn't show.*'"

"Disappointment is common in lots of divorces, but in yours, it was constant, huh?"

"Yes, unfortunately, it was a very common occurrence. It was very difficult to watch the girls get their hopes up and then be disappointed again and again and again. It wasn't fair; they didn't ask for this divorce. You know? It broke my heart each and every time."

"Yes, I can imagine. Did he show up that evening?"

"Yes. I was outside putting the cover on the pool when I heard the sliding glass door open, and Kevin and Chloe walked out. I waved hello, and I could see Chloe's smile from ear to ear. Her dad was here. Her dad! God, how she loved her dad. Our conversation was light—the weather, the dog, the new walkway I put out on the front of the house. He asked if I needed help with the pool or with the house—whatever I needed, he would come over and put the filter away. His nonchalant attitude and ability to stroll in and out of our lives really pissed me off. I knew it was his guilt talking. He was trying to make up for lost time."

"No opportunity to make up from your perspective?"

"Nope. That was when I lost it."

"You've been pretty calm up to this point, staying positive around the relationship. What do you mean you lost it?"

"Without warning, I turned to him and screamed—literally, screamed (and I'm not a screamer), 'I don't need for you to stroll back into our lives and try to make everything all right. It's not going to happen. I needed to be loved, to be sheltered, to be cared for, to have a partner in my life. I needed someone to talk to, to hang out with, to laugh and cry with. I can stand alone; I've stood alone. I have screwed in light bulbs, cleaned gutters, and removed a jam from a clogged garbage disposal. I've showed strength and courage to the girls when it was only fear I felt. I've wiped tears, mowed the lawn, used the snow blower in a blizzard, tilled the garden, stayed up late with barfing children and a dog with the shits. I've provided hugs when they needed them and provided discipline when it was necessary. I've managed my career, I've managed my home, and I've managed our girls. I've been responsible and accountable with a plan, a goal, and a focus to make the best for the girls out of the worst that was delivered. Don't you dare think you are going to walk back into my life when you have time or feel the need to offload some guilty feelings. Don't act like you are here to save me from my chores and my challenges. I needed you, and you were not there for me. Now, I can do it myself, and when I can't, I will ask those people in my life who were always there for me. So, *fuck you!*'"

"Ouch!"

"Yeah. You said it.

"I turned back into the house and continued with my chores. He stood there speechless. There was nothing he could have said that I'd listen to. Nothing. He spent time with the girls and then left again. Turns out this time, he would be gone for a very, very long time.

"The holidays were tough that first year—both Thanksgiving and Christmas. It was weird for all of us to know that our family structure had changed; however, I decided that I would continue with all of the normal traditions we held dear to our hearts every year. It was important for the girls to know that life goes on. I've always felt strongly that traditions ground families—whether it's simply the same dish every Thanksgiving or the annual family gathering. We may have taken an unexpected hit, but we were going to survive and flourish. The whole family—my parents, sister, brother-in-law, and brother came over to our home for Thanksgiving, and we decorated the tree in the afternoon as we had done every year before. Christmas Eve was at our home, and we celebrated with the traditional Polish meal. On Christmas morning, Grandma and Grandpa came over for breakfast and to watch the kids open presents. Around lunch, we headed to my sister's for Christmas dinner and the celebration of both Chloe's and my birthdays.

"Instead of being sad on New Year's Eve, I decided to reflect on the year and write a letter to those who supported me throughout the first tough year."

"Did you keep the letter?"

"Yes, I can share it with the audience if you'd like. As you can see, it has been yellowed, tattered, and torn from the years of wear in my wallet."

"Please, read it out loud. I can't believe you've kept that folded-up note for so long! Why did you keep it?"

"I meant every word I said in that letter. I guess I kept it so I wouldn't forget how that New Year's Eve felt."

"This is my letter to my friends and family: 'December 31, 2004. It's New Year's Eve, a day to reflect on the past year and to anticipate the start of the New Year. It seems fitting that as I reflect on 2004, I send you a note of thanks for being a special part of my life.

"'I never imagined that I would be divorced—but that's what life is. It's an unexpected journey where we cannot see the future. During this year, you have played a very important part of my journey—probably more than you even know. You were there for me when I needed to talk, cry, or be hugged. You were there for me when there was laughter, joy, and happiness. You were there for me when I needed help, support, or encouragement. You were there for me with your prayers and your strength to guide me along.

"'I've learned many lessons this year, and I hope my daughters have learned many lessons from me through my actions. I've learned that I never want to change the oil in my lawnmower or snow blower, that a washing machine tub filled with water that cracks can create quite a flood (and that eventually everything will dry out!), that it requires strength and courage to recognize when you need help and it's OK to ask for it, that family and friends will rally around you to get you through the tough times, that is it cheaper to replace the lawn-mower string than to buy a new lawnmower (as long as you ask your dad for help!), and that no matter how bad you want to, you cannot control the actions of others; you can only control your own. I've been reminded what life's priorities are: if it's a choice between playing a game with the girls or cleaning, it's the game I choose; the dust can wait. I've learned that the girls can help more with the chores, but that they are still kids and should not bear additional work due to the decisions I have made. I've learned that taking the garbage out to the curb every week is disgusting and is really a guy's job that I just hate! I've learned to take care of myself more and, most important, that life is to be enjoyed—to celebrate each moment, for we truly do not know what tomorrow will bring.

"'I end the year with no regrets and start the year with optimism and hope of what opportunities life will bring me. I'm glad that I married Kevin, and I'm glad that we shared sixteen years and had two beautiful children. I'm glad that I had the strength and courage to make the choice to file for divorce, and I'm glad that we made it through the most difficult year. I'm thankful that I can wake up every morning to see the sunrise outside my bedroom window, knowing that I have been given a new day to celebrate. But most of all, I am thankful that you are in my life and want you to know that you are very much loved and cherished. I could not imagine this year without you in it. Happy New Year! Love, Stephanie.'"

"That was a beautiful letter. How'd you feel reading it again after all these years?"

"I feel peaceful and proud. When I wrote it, I was thankful, full of hope, and able to breathe again. I knew the road ahead would be challenging, but the old road was not where we needed to be. We had to change paths. Our future was both bright and scary all at once. Making the decision to divorce was only step one on a multi-mile journey. Regardless of the journey's length, we were on our way."

Chapter 12

New Year—New Life

"January 1, 2005, Happy New Year! It was a new year. The initial divorce shock had worn off, and the reality of being a single parent and single was settling in. I had just turned thirty-nine—twelve months to forty. I made a commitment to myself on January 1 that when I reached my fortieth birthday, I would be back in control of every aspect of my life. During the first year after the divorce, I didn't do any dating—purposely. It was a time for everyone to begin to heal and find a new schedule in our lives."

"Forty was a big deal for you?"

"Yes. It was a symbolic turning point in my life. I felt empowered. I felt like I had my 'freedom,' and I knew that I was in control of my fate. I had felt for too long that I wasn't in control of my life, that I was settling for less than I truly deserved. I deserved more, and I was going to take life back—and forty would be the time!

"I had always dreamed of vacationing in Paris with my love, walking the streets hand in hand, kissing along the Seine River. It was romantic and beautiful and a dream I held close. Kevin never liked to travel. It was not something he enjoyed, so all travels were with friends or my family. I promised myself on this day that I would celebrate my fortieth birthday in Paris."

"Tell us about your first year. How'd you get through?"

"I spent time focusing my love, support, and attention on my two best girlfriends, who were experiencing challenges in their lives. Kimberly was in a serious car accident in November 2004 and continued to suffer throughout the year with pain from the accident. She underwent multiple procedures, physical therapy sessions, and challenges at work as she tried to get back on her feet.

"Sandy identified a lump in her breast during the summer. We were at our monthly breakfast when she casually mentioned she'd found something. Both Kimberly and I immediately jumped on her case to get it checked out. Eventually, she went for a mammogram. Unfortunately, it turned out to be cancer. It was a long, tough battle for her to try to shrink the tumor, and when that was not successful, she had a mastectomy and then went through eight weeks of radiation—losing all of her hair and some of her dignity and femininity. She pulled through and successfully beat her cancer, and Kimberly and I were right by her side as we fought the battle together, as only good friends could."

"It must've been difficult as you're trying to get your feet under yourself with your new life and assisting and supporting your two best friends through the most difficult challenges they faced. How'd you all cope?"

"It's all about being a friend. We spent a lot of time with each other, laughing and crying. We got through it together. I knew if there was a time when I needed them as much as they needed me, they would have done the same, no questions asked. Over the years we established a relatively frequent wine-night to get together. Sometimes it would be a '*whine-night*' but it was always a wine night. Those gatherings kept us all sane as we went through each of our individual battles.

"The other thing I did in 2005 was to slowly purchase all new furniture, new accessories, dishes, etc."

"Why?"

"It was my opportunity to remove all of the items in my home that reminded me of Kevin. It was a cathartic experience, and as the old moved out, the new moved in, which provided just a little bit more closure each time a change occurred. I needed to have a happy home—happy memories, not sad. Can you guess what went first?"

"Hmmm…bedroom set?"

"No. Actually the couch was the first thing to go when I had the money. Removing it from my home helped heal the pain and sadness of what that couch represented. Remember, for so many years, he laid and slept there. It represented laziness, hurt, anger, rejection. Lucky I didn't burn the damn thing!"

"Did you keep your bedroom set?"

"Yes, he rarely slept there, so it didn't bother me."

"At this time, did you learn about all the details about what happened with Kevin? Everything he did?"

"No. It was now the end of 2005, and there were still many things I didn't know about what Kevin did and the timing. I don't know when or how he lost his brand-new Ford F-150 pickup truck, and I don't know exactly how many times and in what manner he tried to kill himself. And for the first time, I couldn't care any longer. It's weird, I cared because he was our daughters' father, but I didn't care for me any longer. Does that make sense?"

"Yes, I think I understand. It was a different kind of caring and more distant."

"Yes, that's correct."

"Were the kids seeing their father?"

"During this year, the kids didn't see much of Kevin. He was in and out of severe depression, in and out of the hospital, and in and out of work. It was horribly tough for the girls and emotionally difficult for all of us to handle. Imagine how you would feel every time you were promised something at the age of fifteen or eleven, and then it was taken away. That's what the girls felt every time they waited for Kevin to show up when he promised he would. Their hearts broke a little more each time. My heart felt their pain, and there was nothing I could do to prevent the hurt from happening. All I could do was to be there and provide them with the support they needed to lessen the pain. I couldn't make it go away. As a mom, it was hard to watch and not be able to help."

"Were there times when you were regretting the divorce to spare the kids the disappointment they were feeling now?"

"Maybe a minute or two here and there but not much. I knew that if we were still all together, the girls would be learning more about how a relationship is *not* supposed to be and they would have different disappointments they would be dealing with. So, overall, no.

"I could only help with what I had control of. That became my mantra. Could I control it? Could I change it? If the answer was no, I focused on changing my attitude. That was all I had. That's all each of us has. Recognizing this was so important in keeping a positive attitude."

"You could control your feelings and what you said about Kevin. How did you manage not to slam him on every opportunity you had?"

"I remained as supportive as possible and never said anything bad about Kevin to the girls. What I said under my breath and what I said to my girlfriends was a whole different story! I tried very hard to understand depression so that I could put myself in Kevin's shoes and help the girls. It was tough for me. I can't understand it because I've never experienced it. I'll admit that was a challenge and has continued to be a challenge because it's so foreign to everything I know about positive thinking."

Chapter 13

The Year of Doug and Broken Promises

"When did you have your first significant relationship?"

"Two thousand six was when I had my first post divorce boyfriend."

"What was his name?"

"Doug."

"Would you describe him for us?"

"Sure. He was very nice and cute. A true gentleman with a great sense of humor. He always opened the door for the female co-workers, which was not something you see very frequently in today's culture. Perhaps it was his southern upbringing. I think his momma raised him right. He had brown hair and brown eyes and was about 3 inches shorter than me. He was the first and only guy I ever dated where I was taller. I learned to wear flats when we were together.

"How long did you date?"

"It was about eight months of actual dating. We knew each other for about a year before we began dating."

"How'd you meet?"

"I was the project manager for our company for a large outsourcing initiative, and he was hired by our vendor to manage the project on their side. We met at work."

"How'd it move from the professional relationship to a realization that you both wanted more?"

"There was always flirting between us. However, during a weeklong trip to Florida for the project implementation planning, we went out for dinner one night with the project team. Doug drove me back to my hotel, and we began to talk about the fact that we were getting close to the end of our project and that Doug's yearlong contract was going to be up. He was joking about how he would have his 'get out of jail free card.' As we pulled up to the hotel, I turned to him and asked, 'Is that when you will finally kiss me?' To my utter surprise, his response was yes."

"Just like that?"

"Just like that. I was speechless. I think I almost peed myself from surprise. All I could mutter out was 'Really?' I had hoped for that response but did not expect to get it. We gave each other a good-bye hug, and as I got out of his car and went into the hotel, I could feel the grin across my face—ear to ear! I felt him watch me walk into the hotel, and before entering the spinning doors, I turned, waved, and blew him a good-bye kiss. As if I was floating on cloud nine, I found my way to my room and slept with sweet dreams. I think I may have actually skipped a little on my way inside the hotel. *What was I twelve?*"

"What happened when you returned to Connecticut?"

"We continued to work on our project and began to talk about how we felt about each other. I asked him how long he had felt we could be more than 'friends,' and he said he'd thought that about me almost immediately from the day we met."

"In February, I flew down to Florida to surprise Doug for his birthday. It was supposed to be the bunch of us going out to dinner, and we had concocted this elaborate plan for two of my additional project coworkers from Florida, Jill and Jack, to take Doug out to dinner. The plan was that when they arrived at the restaurant, I would show up unexpectedly. Unfortunately, Jill and Jack got stuck in Connecticut because of the project deliverables and couldn't get back, so the day before his birthday, I called Doug's office and asked if he had plans for dinner on his birthday. He said he was planning to go with Jack but since he could not get back from Connecticut, that he didn't have any plans. I asked if he wanted to go with me. He said, 'You're kidding. You're actually coming down to Florida?'

"When I said, 'Yes, I am.' He was speechless. Five hours later, I was getting on a plane."

"Did you move your relationship forward during that visit?"

"Yes and no."

"He picked me up at my hotel around four thirty in the afternoon, and we headed to the beach for a drink at our favorite beachside bar and a romantic stroll along the coast. It was a beautiful evening around 50 degrees; there were tons of stars in the sky, and we stopped to look at the ring around the full moon. I made a comment about how beautiful the evening was, and Doug turned to me and said that this was a perfect day and there was only one thing that would make the night perfect. He then pulled me close to him. Our bodies touched, and he kissed me. As we separated from each other, he said that now the night was perfect—with a perfect kiss."

"So, you got the first kiss during a romantic beach stroll?"

"Yes. Right out of the pages of a great romance novel. You can't make this stuff up! There is nothing more fantastic than that first kiss. I commented that I wondered if he was ever going to kiss me. I was dying! He asked if he had waited too long and then followed up to say he wanted the moment to be perfect. He picked a great time. It was wonderfully romantic with the waves crashing against the shore under a full moon. We walked hand in hand with smiles across our faces back to his car and drove the twenty minutes back to his house. It was three in the morning before we stopped kissing on his couch and decided that it was best he drive me back to the hotel.

"He called into work late the next morning to pick me up at the hotel around nine and head out to breakfast before he dropped me off at the airport and I flew home."

"You didn't stay the night with him?"

"No. It would have been too risky for our jobs. We still had a few months to work together before we completed our project. We couldn't add complexities to what was already becoming a steamy relationship."

"Our newfound romance was interrupted with some bad news. Doug's dad passed away unexpectedly in March. I had a feeling that something wasn't right when he hadn't heard from his dad for a few days and was unable to reach him. I had been out shopping with the girls on a Sunday afternoon when I received the call. As soon as I heard his voice, I already knew there was something wrong. I pulled the car to the side of the highway to hear him say his dad had died. Doug was in Kentucky. He had flown out as quickly as he could. As he choked the tears back, my tears flowed down my cheeks. My heart broke for him. I just wanted to hold him and let him know it would be OK, but I couldn't. The first thing he did was to thank me for convincing him to go to home for Christmas. It turned out that was his last Christmas with his dad, and I can't imagine how difficult it would have been for him had he not had his Christmas memories."

"Did you force him to go to Kentucky for Christmas?"

"You can't force someone to do something. I learned that with Kevin. We talked about it, and I strongly encouraged him. Family is more important than work, and he typically put work first. He was one of those businessmen who would always put work first. He finally realized that no matter how important the project was, he would go home for the holiday. It was the last time he would see his father."

"Did you fly to Kentucky?"

"I thought about it seriously and even talked to my boss about taking a few days and going but decided not to. We did talk almost daily. I was the only one he could share his feelings with. He had to be strong for his mom and sister. He didn't have to be strong with me."

"Did your daughters know about Doug?"

"Yes. They knew we were friends and that we worked together on this large project I was managing. They also knew when he came up to Connecticut we would go out, and every few months when I needed a break from the reality of life, I would fly to Florida to hang out with Jill and Doug."

"How do you think they were handling the fact that you had someone in your life who could potentially be a long-term relationship?"

"I don't think they thought of it that way. Doug lived in Florida. It was far away. They weren't thinking he would be coming to Connecticut, and neither did I."

"So, he wasn't a risk to your family dynamics?"

"No."

"When did you see him again?"

"April. My team and I pulled an all-nighter on March 31 to ensure our systems went live as planned. It was flawless, and we ended one day earlier than expected. I flew back down to Florida on April 1 to ensure we were prepared for the April 3 go-live."

"Did you spend every moment together?"

"We enjoyed the rest of the week together—worked and flirted together during the day (he loved the way I looked in my skirts and business suits) and then spent the evenings together eating dinner, walking the beach, hanging out, and enjoying each other's company. It was dreamy—all that I could have expected. It was sexy too. No one knew what our relationship was except us. Could there be speculation? Sure...but nothing confirmed. It was our own little secret. It was fun. It was during this trip that our relationship moved to the next level *(if you know what I mean)*. Before that week was out, we planned our next trip—New York City for May."

"You saw each other every few months during 2006?"

"Yes, that's pretty much what our long-distance relationship ended up being. We kept in touch through work and personal calls as well as e-mails between visits but were clearly focused on the next time we would be together.

"It was a great weekend trip. We went with another couple and had a blast. We saw everything you could see in New York—Ground Zero, Central Park (we went on a romantic horse and buggy ride), Strawberry fields; we took a tour of the city on a double-decker bus, got caught in a huge rainstorm and soaked down to our bones. We dressed up one evening in our finest (my little black dress and his handsome suit) and enjoyed *The Phantom of the Opera* with dinner following at the Four Seasons Restaurant, and another night, we ate under the stars at

Tavern on the Green. New York City is a romantic place to be when you're smitten with someone."

"Were you falling in love?"

"I loved Doug. Part of me knew that our distance would never really work out, and I focused a lot of energy to suppress those thoughts. I needed to let the relationship just flow and not analyze every aspect and plan too far into the future. For once, I just enjoyed the moments for what they were—nothing more."

"You didn't answer my question."

"Yeah, I know. I'm trying to dodge it. I think at the time, I thought I was in love with Doug, but in retrospect, I loved him. I can see I was not in love with him. Doug was not a PDA kind of guy."

"PDA?"

"**P**ublic **D**isplay of **A**ffection—no hugging, kissing, holding hands in public? I'm a mushy-gushy, snuggling kind of girl."

"Was that an issue?"

"Yes, for me, it was. I'm gushy. Not like we would be making out on the streets. No one wants to see that! But there's nothing wrong with holding hands, hugging, stealing a kiss in public. By the end of this New York trip, he was holding hands in public, and one night, we ran out to a martini bar at three in the morning, and under the bright lights of the Chrysler Building, he gave me one hell of a stupendous kiss. Big step for him."

"And by the end of the trip...?"

"We planned our next getaway—for July."

"It's like your relationship was a series of mini vacations. Is that how it felt?"

"In retrospect, yes, they were getaways from my responsible life to enjoy time to just be a woman. Not a mom, not a boss, not a disciplinarian, not an organizer, just a single woman hanging out with a guy who adored her. I think it was also good for the girls to get a break from me."

"Tell us about the July trip."

"Our weekend started with drinks at our favorite Beach Bar—at the Jacksonville beach area—followed by a walk on the beach, kissing and holding hands. We always started our trips this way—unwinding, watching the seagulls and listening to the rhythm of the waves crashing on the shore."

"Little more PDAs, huh?"

"Yes, he was getting it! We had dinner at the Dolphin restaurant with a gentle rain falling outside. The restaurant was romantic and dark. Doug started every dinner together with a romantic toast to our time together and how glad he was that I was there with him. After the toast, he held my hand to his lips and gently kissed it. During the conversation, he asked if my eyes were green as he gently rubbed his hand across my cheek and stroked his thumb gently over my hands. It was a beautiful evening together with a delicious dinner and romantic mood and talk.

"We returned to his home, and as we got into more comfortable clothes, Doug lit the candles and opened a bottle of wine. We cuddled on the couch listening to romantic music. Next morning, we left early to head to Orlando where we stayed at a five-star resort hotel. He did a good job picking out a romantic getaway with our room overlooking the lake and a balcony off the back to experience the ambiance of the resort. After settling into our room, we headed to Universal Studios. We had a blast there during the day and returned to the hotel in the evening. As we got closer to the hotel, you could hear the romantic Italian music, and soon, we dropped our bags and danced under the bright glow of the full moon on the shore of the simulated Italian seaside village to Van Morrison's 'Moon Dance.'

"It was one of those perfect moments, a moment where everything felt right—right place, right time, right moment, and right guy. It was a moment when you felt your heart overflowing because you are both blessed and loved.

"After the dance and the long, sweet, tender kiss, we separated from each other, looked into each other's eyes, and just smiled. We slowly linked our fingers together and walked towards our hotel room. By then, it was after four in the morning. We changed out of our clothes and snuggled into each other's arms, and he held me close with our legs intertwined and my arm across his chest, wrapped tightly to him. After passionate lovemaking, we slowly drifted off to relive the day in our dreams.

"As I packed my bag the next morning in preparation to return to Connecticut, Doug handed me a few CDs that he'd made for me."

"CDs? What was on them?"

"I didn't know. Just tucked them into my purse, and we headed to the airport. Our drive to the airport was quiet as we held hands and reflected on how much we enjoyed our time together. As we said our good-byes at the side of the US Air terminal, we knew it would be a while before we saw each other again. The kiss was passionate and wonderful, and for the first time, I felt sadness as I was leaving. Tears welled in my eyes. I blinked them back and hoped he didn't see. As he'd exited the car, I'd left a card on his seat that he would get when I was already gone. It just said thanks for the wonderful weekend! I didn't know if he felt the same, but I knew I was getting more involved in how I felt about him. His touch and his kiss were meaning more and more. I was falling for him, and for the first time, I really felt that I could be totally loved again. My flight landed on time, and as soon as I located my car in the airport parking garage and called home to let them know I was on the way, I popped in one of the CDs Doug burned for me, and to my surprise, it was love songs. I was so freaked out and thought that perhaps he couldn't say what he was feeling and instead decided to document the songs as his way to share his feelings. I, like so many other girls have probably done, called my girlfriend, popped in a CD, put the phone close to the speaker, and got a second opinion."

"And, what did the girlfriend network report?"

"Many beautiful love songs were on the CDs. In the mix was a song called 'Green Eyes,' which was one of the most meaningful when you truly listened to the words. After listening, I knew why he asked if my eyes were green during our romantic dinner. I listened to the words, and it was like he was sharing his feelings directly with me. He wasn't able to communicate his feelings verbally. He communicated his feeling through music.

"If you've never heard it, it's a beautiful song. Let's play the song. Pay close attention to the words in the chorus. It's a great song.

The audience sat quietly and the song began slowly and grew louder and louder until the audience was mesmerized. With about 250 of the 300 seats filled with women, you can feel the emotion in the room as they were hanging on every word, listening to the meaning and imagining they were receiving those words from someone in their own life. Each person in that audience was engaged, was involved and felt the love I felt that night when I first listened to that song. *It's as if I was hearing the song for the first time. It brought me back to a warm and loving place.*

"Later that month, the girls and I went to Maine for our annual family vacation, and I spent time thinking of Doug while I was walking along Wells Beach. There wasn't a day that he didn't cross my mind. As I walked along the water's edge, I looked down and saw a heart-shaped rock. Many wouldn't think it meant anything. For me, I took it as a sign that although we were far away, our hearts were somehow connected. OK, so I am sappy like that. That evening, I wrote a poem about those feelings. I never gave Doug the poem, and I shared it with no one. I thought of sending the poem and rock to Doug but never did. It sat on my bedroom bureau for months until, along with all other Doug items, it was boxed up. In retrospect, I believe I never sent it because I didn't think that Doug would appreciate the poem. I wrote the words wanting the feelings to be real but somehow deep down in my heart, knowing they weren't and I wasn't going to open up my heart to pain again."

"It sounds as if you were back and forth with the emotions. Not quite sure if you should give in to the feelings and risk getting hurt or just have some fun and let it go on its own path knowing it was short-lived."

"Yes, it was a reflective vacation. That's something I find the ocean brings to you—reflection. I began to wonder if I was settling for something that could never really meet my needs. Was I settling for the vision of love and filling in the blanks where things were missing? I wasn't ready to admit out loud my thoughts, but they were swirling in my mind."

"Do you still have the poem? Will you share it?"

"Yes, I have the paper folded in my purse—I brought it with me in case we got on this topic."

Let me grab it and read it to everyone.

Heart of the Sea

Looking out upon the sea, waves crash into shore
Lovers walk hand in hand—sharing laughter and joy
Remembering your hand in mine, fingers tightly intertwined
Wonder if you are on the sand, watching the waves—daydreaming of me
Waves crash upon my toes—looking down a heart appears
A reminder I choose to believe—although a thousand miles away—hearts connected by dreams and waves crashing upon the shore of the same sea.

"That is a beautiful poem. Never sent it, huh?"

"Never even told him about it."

"Guess he knows now, huh?"

"Yes, he knows now if he happens to be watching this interview. There seem to be multiple first-time learnings happening during the show today."

"When did you see him again?"

"August. I was in town for one night visiting another company I was doing business with."

"Did you guys connect?"

"Yes. I had big dreams of the time we'd spend together. A wonderful, romantic, amazing night."

"How'd that work for you?"

"Yeah, not exactly as I had imagined. Went something like this: Doug picked me up from the hotel around five in the evening, and we headed to the beach for our traditional drink at the beachside bar, dinner, and a walk. We both very much looked forward to this time together. After we enjoyed ourselves at the beach, we headed back to Doug's house. We entered through the garage and into the kitchen. Doug went upstairs for a moment—probably to pee—and I noticed that the picture of us together on his birthday that had been on the fridge since February was no longer there. The only picture there was Doug next to the Wall Street Bull from our May trip."

"Did you ask him where it went when he came downstairs?"

"No, I didn't say anything. I felt so hurt I didn't want to speak but could feel the wave of rejection coming over me. It was a sign that I wasn't really ready to see. I knew he was very stressed out at work, and I knew I was not his priority or focus during the ten hours I was with him that day. I was making excuses. I thought, Wow, I'm once again not someone's priority. I'm off the fridge! WTF? W...T...F? Oh yes, WTF—What the fuck?

"Although we enjoyed our time together that evening relaxing on the couch and watching romantic movies, it felt strained."

"Did you stay the night?"

"No. I couldn't stay at his house because I was with a coworker."

"Did he offer to join you at your hotel?"

"No."

"Hmmm"

"Yeah, I know. You don't need to say anything more—I know. What guy wouldn't stay the night?"

"In my heart, I knew that if someone really wanted or loved you, they would want to spend time together; they'd figure out how to make it happen. I made excuses in my mind, justifications, and rationalizations. I didn't ask him about that picture during my trip or why he didn't stay with me. There were some things I couldn't comfortably discuss with him. He didn't offer up conversations like this, and I found sometimes it was uncomfortable to discuss feelings with him."

"So, you left Florida and returned home pissed?"

"More hurt than pissed—and confused.

"When I returned to Connecticut and began to tell the story to my girlfriends, they asked me if the relationship was enough for me. Was I getting the love and attention I wanted or deserved? When we were together, it was always nice, but the question was really whether the time apart would hold us together until the next time we got together? My girlfriends felt I was settling. One thing you can always appreciate is the honesty of your girlfriends.

"It was a good question and one I really didn't want to face. Rejection again would be tough to handle—for anyone. Even for me. But, on the other hand, I knew I couldn't settle for less than I deserved. I'd been down that path before."

"You're no longer working together on the project at this time, right? So, it's just a personal relationship?"

"Correct."

"When was your next trip?"

"September. This was a longer trip than one of our regular week-end getaways. It was five days, and we were going to the Bahamas.

"The time came quickly, and soon I was packing my bags with all kinds of thoughts running through my head. Our relationship was becoming strained—and I had serious doubts as to whether to spend the five days away from the girls if the relationship would end after this trip. But, on the flip side, a break from the responsibility routine for the girls and me was a good thing.

"I packed up and talked to Doug the night before I left to ensure we had everything covered that we needed to bring, and then I tried to sleep and woke early the next morning to catch a plane. It was roman-tic, I had to admit—it had been five weeks since we'd seen each other, and we almost had to cancel the trip due to Doug's work commit-ments. However, at the last moment, he actually chose me over work. That was a miracle—first time that had happened during the length of our relationship. I thought, *OK, this is a good sign. This will be a good trip.*

"We both flew to Miami International Airport. His flight was to arrive at eight forty-five and mine was to arrive at nine that morning, and then we would depart at ten thirty for Nassau. I arrived on time and looked at the flight arrival board to see that he had arrived on time. I headed down to the gate where our next flight was, and about fifteen minutes later, I spotted him coming down the escalator. Our eyes met, and he walked over to where I was sitting and hugged me before we sat down to chat."

"Awkward?"

"No, actually, it was pretty nice. We were on our way to a wonderful, romantic trip."

"Did he pay for your flights?"

"No, it was Dutch all the way. You thinking maybe that was a sign?"

"Perhaps."

"We chatted until our flight was boarding, and then we walked downstairs and onto the tarmac. We stood right outside of the plane as the propellers were fired up, and then we climbed the stairs and settled into our seats. I took the window, and he took the aisle on this small puddle-jumper—propeller plane. We held hands as we got comfortable with my head on his shoulder, and the plane took off. Both of us napped during the short flight and arrived promptly in Nassau on time. As we began our descent, you could see the unbelievable blue-green waters of the Caribbean.

"We were in our hotel by one and got into our shorts and headed down to the water's edge where we just sat for a few minutes and soaked up the sea air and the spray of the salt water. We were in paradise.

"We decided to take the jitney into town that afternoon and spent hours sightseeing on a horse-and-buggy ride around town. We had a great couple days on the island. It was fun and romantic. We rented a scooter—Doug drove, and I was on the back with my arms wrapped around his waist and the wind whipping through my hair as we drove all over Nassau and Paradise Island. We strolled over secluded beaches and little shops searching for treasures, saw a Junkanoo celebration with brightly colored costumes and a steel band, went out to dinner at romantic beach-front restaurants, played games of checkers on the giant board at the beach, and snuggled under a grass umbrella as the waves crashed along the sea wall under the romantic charm of a full moon.

"The last full day we were there, we decided to take a high-powered speedboat ride to Exuma—an out island. There were only twenty people on this adventure, and we started at Iguana Island. When the boat pulled up, the iguanas came out of the sandy hills to meet us. We fed them grapes on the end of sticks. There were thunderstorms all around us while we were on the island, and in the distance, you could hear the thunder and see lightening, except for right over us, where the sun was shining directly down on us. It was amazing. The dark skies were all around us, and the sun was shining straight down the center of the sky onto the blue-green water. You could see right to the bottom of the water. It was just stunning, and it made me feel like I was in the presence of something so much more powerful than myself.

"After departing there, we headed to the island where we were going to spend our day; we were greeted by the sky opening up and the rains pouring down. As the boat pulled up, you could see the brown dock connected to the restaurant/hut where soon everyone was running for cover. We walked over to the open bar and were greeted by a boar who was traveling down to the beach for a drink of water. I leaned over the edge of the deck and fed the boar carrot sticks…only to be advised by the locals that they could easily chomp my fingers off. I stopped feeding him!

"Soon after we arrived, the skies cleared, and the day was full of adventures, including petting stingrays and feeding sharks. It also included my first experience in snorkeling—it was amazing. The plants, fish, sharks, and stingrays were a beautiful sight as we snorkeled down the ocean back to the main building from the tip of the island. After an authentic Bahamian lunch, we spent the afternoon sitting in the crystal-clear water watching the birds fly overhead and the fish and sharks swim by. It was almost surreal—like something you would hear about in one of Jimmy Buffet's songs."

"Sounds beautiful and very romantic."

"Yes, it was, sitting in the clear water with our bodies touching, the sun on our faces, and the peace and tranquility of the island paradise was picture perfect.

"We left the island late afternoon on a huge cigarette speedboat snuggled together—content and happy with the beautiful day we had experienced. We returned back to pouring rain in Nassau. It apparently had rained the whole day there—a perfect day to be out on an adventure.

"We grabbed a bite to eat that night at a restaurant next door to the hotel and listened to the live band. We headed to the beach to sit for a few minutes on the beach chair before returning to the room. Doug summed up the day by saying that it was the most amazing day he had experienced in his life.

"I started to feel real sick a few minutes after we sat on the beach and knew I had only had that feeling once before in my life. Under the grass hut, the ocean, the sky, and the ground all began to spin."

"Spin? How bad?"

"So bad that I had to close my eyes because I couldn't focus. I wasn't sure I was going to make it back to our room. It was ten times worse than my most horrible motion sickness incident.

"Once I got there, I exploded—out both ends. I wanted to die. I had food poisoning. I'd had it once before. Wished I could die. Doug asked if I wanted him to hold my hair back as I barfed. I declined because there were fluids coming from both ends; it wasn't a pretty sight. I sat in the bathroom until two in the morning before I tried to lie down. Once I lay down, I was up sick again. This continued until three thirty. I didn't know if I was going to be able to make it home on the plane the next day and prayed that I would stop getting sick and could get an hour or two of sleep."

"OK, so let me picture this, you're in paradise on a romantic vacation barfing and pooping your brains out. And where's Doug?"

"In bed…Yeah, he went to bed. Did I mention I thought I was dying? Doug went to sleep—that spoke volumes to me."

"But you said he could go to sleep."

"No, I said I didn't need my hair to be pulled back. He should have stayed up with me.

"I finally fell asleep and woke around eight the next morning feeling like death. We went downstairs. Doug got some breakfast, and I picked up some crackers. Not sure how I did it, but I made it home on the flight that day.

"We flew back to Florida together and decided on our flight to order a pizza in for dinner so that we could just chill on the couch, watch a movie, and enjoy our last night together. I debated whether to bring up the conversation about where we went from there, so I didn't. He didn't bring up plans for our next trip, and neither did I. Maybe part of me already knew there would not be one.

"That night, before we settled into bed, I did ask where our picture that was on the fridge went. He said he took the pictures down for one of the cleaning lady trips since she was scrubbing down the fridge. He said it must just not have made its way back up—yet the picture of him with the Wall Street bull had. Interesting. I told him he didn't need to put it back up…He pulled it out of the junk drawer and put it back up. That pissed me off. It was in the junk drawer? Jeez!"

"Lying?"

"I thought so. Could it have been true? Sure, but my gut told me he was taking the pieces of our lives and putting them away slowly. And for once, it was a sign I saw with eyes wide open.

"I turned and walked upstairs and got ready for bed. The next morning, we didn't make love before I left."

"Another sign?"

"Yes. That was my doing. I wasn't going to give more of me when I wasn't going to get it back.

"We cuddled, and then I packed and he brought me to the airport. It wasn't like other departures. This one felt different. I think we both knew that our relationship would never be more than good friends with benefits.

"When I landed in Connecticut that morning, I turned on my cell phone and had a message from Doug. It wasn't like him to call me so I was excited but skeptical. He just left a message to call him.

"When Doug picked up, all he said was that Steve (his mother's significant other) was found dead that morning by a friend. His mom was out of town visiting his sister in Kentucky.

"So much for having a nice vacation. Everything changed again. Another tragedy for Doug to deal with.

"I had another moment of clarity right there in the middle of the US Air terminal at Bradley International Airport in Hartford, Connecticut, at seven on a Sunday evening. I was placed in Doug's life for a very specific reason and he in mine. It was so apparent to me right then and there. Everything was going to change between us."

"So, you had a wonderful time, but you already knew it was the end?"

"Yes. It was a wonderful friendship that turned into more. And for the time we enjoyed each other and a romantic relationship, it was what we both needed in our lives at that time. In my head, I knew there was no real future. In my heart…that was a sad reality overcoming my heart.

"The following weekend we had the 'break up' discussion.

"It doesn't matter whether you're eighteen and breaking up or if you're thirty-nine and breaking up, the feelings are still the same, and you end up going through all of the same emotions. The only difference is that you realize you're not going to die over the relationship and that your heart cannot physically break.

"Even though I felt that we may not be together forever, it was still difficult to have someone not want me any longer. I began to cry as he explained why it was time for us to go our separate ways. Some of the key points of the conversation included: He wanted a family, and I'd already had one. We lived far away from each other and wouldn't be able to be together for years. He wanted me in his life; I was the angel who helped him get through the toughest year of his life. I was his best friend, and he couldn't imagine not having me in his life, but he didn't want me enough to commit."

"So, you would have had more kids and possibly moved to Florida?"

"No, that would have been a negative on both. But it's weird how when you're in the middle of a breakup, you can just about justify anything— and I know that's what I was doing. Well, that's what my logical side was doing. It was trying to stop my heart from breaking. I was *almost* willing to say or do whatever not to end the relationship—that was my heart talking. In retrospect, I would never have moved, but in the heat of the relationship or the pending knowledge that it might all end, I may have convinced myself that I would do just that."

"So, did you step back and think rationally about it?"

"You know, when you want something to work out so badly that even though you know it probably shouldn't or couldn't, deep down inside, you wish and wish and pray it could. That's how I felt. It sucked.

"It took quite a few weeks of talking and crying with girlfriends to be OK. Thank God for my girlfriends. They continue to be an area of strength in my life to get through the tough times."

"Well, I guess it was no Paris, France, with a special guy for your fortieth birthday?"

"Nope! It was time to kick in the backup plan."

"When did you see Doug again?"

"It was actually May of 2007 when I went down to visit my girlfriend Jill for a weekend. That was the last time I saw Doug. It was also the same weekend I first communicated with my future husband. Weird, huh? We'll get to that in a few minutes."

"So, you've been dumped. Now what are you thinking?"

"Guys suck!"

"What were your plans for dating?"

"For a while, do nothing, regroup, rejuvenate, reflect, be OK alone. I was always OK being without a partner who didn't complete me. I knew I would never be alone in my life. I had my girls. I had my girlfriends. I had my family. They would always be there for me. I would always be there for them.

"I was placed in Doug's life to weather the difficult loss of his father and the challenges in finding a balance between love and money. Doug was placed in my life to be my transition relationship, to help me regain my confidence, to remember all that I have to give to a man and for me to learn what I want and don't want from a relationship.

"We each learned and grew from our time together—and that is a wonderful thing."

"Such a positive attitude for being dumped."

"It's been a few years now so the pain isn't as sharp and biting as it was before."

"Where's Kevin during these eighteen months?"

"Not in the girls' lives."

"Nothing? No contact, no calls, no nothing?"

"No. Just the girls and me. We had no idea where he was. We were OK."

Chapter 14

Cocaine and a Tattoo

"On October 5, I booked my trip to Paris to celebrate my fortieth birthday—Paris Hotel in Las Vegas, that is. Nothing like planning a big trip to get a guy off your mind. No idea yet who would be going with me. I would be OK to go alone, but it would be a lot more fun to go with someone who could celebrate life alongside me. Someday, I would get to France with a man I loved right beside me smooching and kissing all over Paris! Not now, but someday.

"Along with trying to move through the emotions of the breakup, life still went on—no time to have a pity party. I kept myself busy over the month by enjoying my first spa day with my prior boss, running Chloe to basketball practice, coaching the junior high cheerleading squad, getting our family portrait done, and keeping my head above water at work. This new staffing position included a staff of ten, two million-dollar contracts I was negotiating, and implementing many high-profile projects. I was busy. It kept my mind occupied, and for that, I was grateful.

"I asked my girlfriends Jill and Lisa to spend my birthday in Vegas with me, and they agreed. So, we began to plan. It was November 10 that my girlfriend Lisa and I went shopping for our 'birthday dresses' for the Vegas trip. It was a total girl day as we grabbed armfuls of gowns and dresses from the racks at the high-end department stores and headed into the dressing room where we tried on one dress at a time. It was hysterical as I came out in the poufy red 'prom' dress and then the black 'slutty' dress as well as the ten other dresses that just didn't look right, including a long, white sequined gown; a satin turquoise dress with a bow on the side; and a skintight tea length. We had decided to leave the blue velvet dress for last. We picked it off the rack because it reminded Lisa of a Christmas long ago when her mom and dad got all dressed up for a party and her mom wore a beautiful blue velvet dress.

"When I pulled the velvet dress on, it was stunning. With my green eyes and blond hair, the dress just popped. As soon as I left the dressing room, Lisa agreed that this was the dress.

"After paying, we headed down to the shoe department to purchase my first sexy ankle-strap high-heel shoes. I'd never owned a pair, and Lisa said that as soon as I wore them, I would immediately feel beautiful. She was right. I slipped them on and strutted around in my jeans and high-heel shoes—it was amazing. They were purchased, and we were stoked for our trip.

"The next morning at work, the red light was on my phone, and it was a message from my mom. You know it's going to be a tough phone call when it starts with: 'There's no good time, place, or way to deliver this message.' I immediately knew it was about Kevin. For some reason, my mom and sister felt they needed to continue to protect me from Kevin. I already knew in my heart that he was using again.

"My mom confirmed that after calling Kevin's brother, she found out he was again using cocaine. He lost his job, lost his truck, and was kicked out the house he shared with his girlfriend. He was in a homeless shelter. My heart sank to the pit of my stomach. The thought of having to have this conversation with the girls almost made me vomit. I could feel my anxiety growing and the tears forming as I tried to keep it together and get through the rest of the day's meetings. It was a very tough morning and early afternoon. I was angry, scared, and worried—angry that I had to hurt the girls again, angry that any hope of financial help with Courtney's college education was up Kevin's nose and once again the world was on my shoulders, and worried and scared for how this would impact the girls."

"You must've just wanted to cry."

"I did cry. That night, I talked to Courtney first. She didn't say much—just rolled her eyes a lot and then said it just figured that this was what Kevin did again. It was too bad because this was the day that she received her first college acceptance from Penn State. Bittersweet. We celebrated her amazing accomplishment. It was a milestone day for her and for me, as her very proud mom.

"When Chloe returned from the boys' basketball game, I sat her down to tell her what was going on. She just rolled her eyes too and said she didn't care anymore. I know that reaction was her defense and I would need to watch her actions, statements, etc., as she dealt with Kevin's issues. My inside voice kept saying, *Don't let her get close to him again. Don't let her get back in contact with him—not for a very long time. She doesn't need to be hurt again. She can't continue to be let in and out of his life at his convenience.* I didn't think Kevin had any idea of the hurt and anger Chloe was feeling. I saw it every day. It broke my heart."

"What kept you up at night?"

"The thought, worry, concern that he was so weak that he would decide to kill himself. That would be extremely selfish of him to do. Although I played out the scenario a hundred times in my head, and I knew I would deal with it, I just hoped it didn't happen for the girls' sake.

"The next morning, I called Kevin's cell phone. We needed a 'come to Jesus' discussion. I told him that until he straightened up his life and dealt with all the demons, got sober and clean, he could not have a relationship with his kids. They were suffering way too much by having him come in and out of their lives. The disappointment was too great. It was tearing them up inside. What I didn't know at that time was that it would be over a year before he would be sober long enough and I would be comfortable that he was stable and could be part of the girls' lives."

"A year? That's a long time to be without a dad."

"In kid time, it was forever!"

"So, you truly became a single parent—no support whatsoever?"

"No support."

"You did something totally out of character that December, didn't you?"

"Yes, it was December 1, 2006. I remember the date. For anyone who knew me, they would never expect it was something I would do. It's not something I'd expect me to do, but it was a very exhilarating experience."

"What was it?"

"A tattoo."

"Seriously?"

"Yes. I almost cancelled the appointment during the week—kept swinging between doing it and not doing it. Go or don't go? Would I feel empowered, or would I feel embarrassed? Would it hurt so bad I'd regret it, or worse, would I get a massive infection, end up in the hospital, and then everyone, including my family would know that I got a tattoo? What to do? *What to do?* Five of my tightest friends knew about my adventure and were supportive and encouraging. They said I should do it. I wanted to do it. I needed to do it.

"It was top secret. No one knew except those friends, and they were sworn to secrecy."

"How'd you decide on what to get for a tattoo?"

"Do you believe there is a greater power that guides you?"

"Yes, I do."

"I do as well. The tattoo design came to me one morning."

"What do you mean it came to you?"

"I just woke up, and I saw the whole tattoo in my mind's eye. It was a vision. I felt like I was being guided to capture this moment forever so that I would never forgot. I got up and drew the design on the pad next to my bed. It was as simple as that. It was so amazing and felt very empowering.

"When I went into the tattoo studio a few weeks later to review the design with the artist, who was called Reach, I was a nervous wreck."

"Reach?"

"Yes. His real name was Miles…but I guess Reach was a cooler name. He was loaded with tattoos. I decided to place it on the lower right side of my stomach—just below my bikini line. Only those I wanted to see it would see it. No one else. God knows I am not wearing bikinis any longer, so the exposure would be limited."

"I think it's amazing that the design came to you in a dream. Tell us about the design."

"A heart was in the center, with a sunrise above the center of the heart, with thirteen rays of different shapes. Off each side of the heart are angel wings with five tips and a shooting star inside the heart. Each part of the tattoo has a special meaning to me."

"Describe for us the design and what it symbolizes."

"The *heart* symbolizes **courage and love.** *It reminds me that I can overcome anything life hands to me. I have made* **it** *through more difficult times during* **twenty years** *than most people face in a lifetime.* It also reminds me that I will someday find love again. I have so much love to give.

"The *sunrise* is for **hope.** *Every day is a new day. We start every day with the hope of a bright tomorrow and the promise of wonder and joy. During the toughest days, looking at the sunrise outside my bedroom window was all I had to kick-start my morning—it's renewal.* It reminds me to be thankful for everything I have and not to dwell on what I don't.

"The *wings* stand for **faith and freedom.** They *remind me that it was my faith that helped me through the darkest times, and it will be my faith to remember that everything happens for a reason. We may not know the reason right now, but one day, we do. It also reminds me that I have the freedom of choice each and every day. There are five tips on each wing. They represent the fingers on each of my hands. This reminds me that we must always give more than we receive in life. There are many people less fortunate that I am. Even at my darkest point, I was blessed. I had family, friends, shelter, and love. There's not more you truly need in life.* The wings of an angel are always watching over me.

"The *shooting star* symbolizes *dreaming. Always, always dream big, set goals in life, and chase those dreams. Don't listen to people who try to knock you down, tell you that you can't succeed, or that you're wrong when*

you know deep down in your soul that you're right. It reminds me to never, ever settle for less than I deserve."

"All the thought and symbolism that went into your tattoo! It's breathtaking and so spiritual."

"Each time I look at it, I am reminded of everything it means to me. I love it."

"Did you go by yourself?"

"Yes, although I thought about bringing one of my girlfriends, I had to do this by myself, for many reasons. I think primarily to prove to myself that I could do this. I could follow my own dream all by myself."

"Did it hurt? Did you cry?"

"Yes, getting a tattoo hurts like a bitch. No, I didn't cry. Believe me that once the pain starts, you feel less of the pain as you go along. You get numb.

"The one thing I didn't realize was what happens after you get the tattoo. The tattoo gets covered in Vaseline and you get wrapped in Saran wrap. Additionally, your tattoo area is swollen. Had no idea that I couldn't sleep on my stomach for almost a week. For the first three days, it was bacitracin on the tattoo every hour, and then for the next week after that, it was lotion once an hour to assist with the healing. Once it all peeled, it was beautiful.

"I gathered up my girlfriends at work into the bathroom one afternoon and proudly showed off the tattoo. Eventually, I showed my friend John, who understands and respects all that I have been through. Wasn't sure how other folks might react. But honestly, I did this for no one but me."

"Did you tell your girls and parents?"

"No. I didn't think my parents or older daughter would approve, and I didn't want to be criticized. I feared telling my younger daughter would drive her to want to get one. The conversation would be something like, 'Do as I say and not as I do'...which I didn't want to say. Eventually, I told them. They found out during a vacation that next spring. Sort of by accident."

"What happened?"

"You know when you sit on the edge of a bed and throw yourself back on the bed?" Well, I did that, and my shirt came up and my pants came down. At the time, I didn't know if anyone saw anything, and I knew it was just a matter of time before someone saw it by accident. So, I decided to tell and show them."

"How'd they react?"

"As I had anticipated. Courtney was like, 'Oh gross,' and Chloe was like, 'Cool, can I get one?' My mother was surprised, and you could tell by the look that she didn't approve. After everyone settled down a little and I composed myself, I explained in detail what the tattoo symbol meant to me. I think at that time, my mother understood a little about why I did the tattoo—a little, but I don't think she fully understood the importance to me since she did not fully understand what I was going through. We've never talked about it further, but I smile every time I look at it."

"Do you think she understands now?"

"I hope so."

"Can you show us? Audience, would you like to see it?"

Applause filled the room as the audience cheered on the tattoo unveiling.

"All right, but everyone has to look beyond the 'muffin top' roll of flab that will come over my pants." As I pulled down my waistband to reveal my tattoo, the audience applauded.

"It's beautiful!"

"Remarkable!"

"Inspiring!"

These were some of the words I heard the crowd exclaim.

"Thanks! I love it! To whomever I choose to share it with, they'll just see a tattoo. But for me, it's my badge of honor. It reminds me of where I've been and where I am going. It reminds me that I can overcome. We can all overcome!

"Previous to getting my own tattoo, I never really understood why it was so important for people to get tattoos. Now I do. I still tell my girls that I won't prevent them from getting a tattoo, but that they should always keep them off their back or neck and arms where either they can be seen with a backless or sleeveless wedding gown or where a new employer can see and judge them."

"Wow. Let's just take a breath before we move on and reflect on that amazing badge of courage. You've shared with us a lot about your family, challenges, and accomplishments. What about your job? During all this, you're still working full-time, right?"

"Yes. My job kept me sane. It gave me the self-confidence that I was missing in other parts of my life. I was needed at work. I was successful. I was considered 'top talent.' It was good."

"Where did you work?"

"I worked at a large insurance company for twenty-five years. I started out as a temporary employee, and over the years, I had the opportunity of leading many amazing projects and working with extraordinary leaders and team members."

"Tell me a little about your career."

"I led the human resource aspect of acquisitions and divestitures, ran an HR contact center, led multiple HR requests for proposals for vendors we outsourced. I've had staffs of five and staffs of up to fifty. I've been the global payroll director at Fortune 100 and Fortune 500 companies and had the opportunity to travel the world. I've had amazing bosses and some of the biggest idiots I've ever met."

"Idiots?"

"Yeah. You know what I'm referring to. Leaders who should never have been placed in positions of responsibility and influence. It's amazing how quickly one person can make or destroy an organization. I've seen both sides of the spectrum. The rise and fall is quick in either direction.

"What I enjoyed most is that throughout my career, I was able to develop myself and my staff. I've been given opportunities to make a difference by supporting the organization's operating plan through some fun activities like hosting a monthly department meeting which addressed specific business topics in a format of a talk show."

"You have your tattoo, you are confident in your career, and you were just about ready to turn forty. What was next for you?"

"My life has just begun. There is so much more to share."

Chapter 15

Forty in Paris (Vegas)

"I picked up Lisa at her house around eleven on that crisp and clear winter morning, and we headed to the airport after a quick drive through Dunkin' Donuts for my coffee and Lisa's iced tea to get the adventure started. We sat at the airport chatting as we waited for the plane to leave. The plane departed on time, and we arrived in Vegas around five thirty that evening after a five-and-a-half-hour flight.

"I was in 'Paris' with two of my very good friends. Happy Birthday to *me*!"

"You knew you really weren't in Paris, though, right? You were in Vegas."

"Yes, of course, but just follow along with my fantasy and you'll see just how much we enjoyed our celebration.

"Jill had already arrived at our hotel around three that afternoon and met us in the lobby of the Paris, Las Vegas, hotel after we arrived. There we stood at the base of the Eiffel Tower; it was very amazing. After settling in to our rooms, we headed out for a quick dinner and drink.

"We turned in early that night, since we'd had a long travel day and we were still on Eastern time, which really messed us up.

"Thursday morning, we woke pretty early—around six thirty and took a run outside on the Strip. It was very windy and chilly, but we walked and ran a mile or two before returning to the hotel, showering, and heading out to breakfast at one of the cafés in the hotel.

"We spent the day strolling in and out of the hotels and shops on the Strip, including the Venetian, Bellagio, Caesar's Palace, Treasure Island, and Paris. After exploring the town, we spent a few hours in the afternoon sitting in the Paris lobby resting and relaxing with an afternoon cocktail. It was so enjoyable not to be anyone's mother, daughter, sister, boss, or coworker for a few days. I could just be me with all the quirks and craziness or laziness I wanted. I was just going to *be*.

"We went to dinner that night at an excellent Italian restaurant in Harrah's called Pazzini where we enjoyed fine wine with an excellent meal. After we finished, we headed to the piano bar in the hotel. Since it was early, they had a karaoke show—featuring Elvis. We settled into a corner table and then moved to directly in front of the stage when a table freed up. We had a blast that night as I was sung to by 'Elvis' and a couple hundred drunk patrons singing 'Happy Birthday.' Lisa and I sang a duet with Elvis to Grease's 'Summer Lovin'.' It was a blast! There was a gentleman sitting next to us who was intrigued by me and dedicated all of his karaoke songs to me. You know, I was loving that. It was some reassurance I needed that someone could find this forty-year-old attractive!

"After the Elvis show was done, the dueling pianos started, and we enjoyed singing along for hours. It was around midnight when we returned to our hotel full of smoke with raspy voices from all of the screeching.

"We woke the next morning to my fortieth birthday. We began at the fitness center, and after completing a four-mile walk/run, we grabbed a bite to eat and then headed to the room. I started to get birthday calls around nine—first from Mom and Dad and then my sister and Chloe. I called home to see if Courtney was good. She reluctantly wished me a happy birthday. *(Gotta love those teenagers!)*

"Around ten thirty, we returned to the spa and picked up our bathrobes and lockers to prepare for our day's treatments. After our relaxing massages, we headed into the salon for our pedicures. We took the top-of-the-line package, and the three princesses sat together in a row of large, brown-leather self-massaging chairs as three lovely ladies pampered our toes. The room was darkened and calming with the smell of lavender around us and the gurgling of the water fountain in the distance.

"It was after three that afternoon when we were done with our showers and blow-drying our hair to return to the room so we could begin to get ready for our six o'clock dinner reservations. Lisa hadn't had a hair updo in years, and since Jill and I were going to wear our hair up, we decided to put Lisa's up also. It was like playing dress-up in high school in preparation for the prom. Lisa finished her makeup before deciding to keep her hair up. She looked very pretty.

"I started to work on my hair and makeup. Around five, I pulled the blue velvet dress over my head and slipped into my black sheer nylons and ankle-strap high-heel black shoes with the tiny white diamond jewels on the strap. I adjusted the sleeves to slip right off each shoulder and put on three-drop diamond earrings and the blue topaz jewel necklace Lisa gave me for my birthday. The girls said I looked stunning. There was a little more cleavage showing than I was normally comfortable with, but I was in Vegas and I felt absolutely beautiful.

"I put on the finishing touches of my makeup and pinned up my hair. It was around five thirty when we were ready to paint the town.

We strutted down the hall in our little black dresses. When we got into the elevator, a gentleman immediately made a comment about how elegant we looked that evening. Of course, the girls said we were celebrating my fortieth birthday, and he commented that I didn't look forty at all. Could've kissed him!

"With a grin on my face and a skip in my step, I headed outside of the hotel and next door to the Arc de Triumph. We took a few group pictures and then some individual pictures. My favorite is me in front of the fountain in my blue velvet dress blowing kisses.

"We headed to the Eiffel Tower restaurant for dinner. The hotel was stunning—even as you begin to rise high into the tower, you get the sense that you will be engaging in an amazing dining experience. The elevator was lined with dark cherry wood walls, and the floor was Italian tiles with a Paris design in the center of the floor. The service from our waiter was excellent. We were treated like queens. The room was dimly lit as we sank into plush red velvet chairs overlooking the Bellagio hotel's water fountain show. We began dinner with a toast of champagne and arugula and poached pear salad and then followed with fresh green beans with toasted almonds, mashed potatoes with cheddar cheese on top, and perfectly grilled steaks. Our dinner ended with an unexpected dessert from the chef of chocolate mousse on a white plate with 'Happy Birthday' written in melted chocolate on the rim of the plate. It was a perfect ending to a perfect dinner.

"Between the champagne toast and the first course, my cell phone rang. When I pulled it from my purse, I saw it was Doug calling. The girls looked at me, and I sent the call to voice mail. I had promised myself that I would no longer be on Doug's time for his convenience in reaching out to me. I would call him back when it was OK for me. After he left his voice message, I heard the phone beep to alert me, and I pulled the phone from my purse again and listened to it. He wished me a happy birthday and said he'd heard a song that day that was about a girl who bought a new dress to celebrate her birthday in Paris. He said it made him think of me. I was happy and sad to get his call. I was happy that he was safely back from his island adventure/trip and sad because it was the final confirmation I needed that we were done. He had confirmed his intentions many weeks ago. I was a little slower, but I knew then, without any shadow of a doubt, we were done. My fortieth birthday was truly the start of many new things. I passed the cell phone to Jill to listen to the message and then to Lisa, and we spent just a few minutes talking about the message he left."

"Must've been a little bittersweet to hear from him."

"Yes, I knew we were done, but I needed to get closure. His call was my closure.

"Lisa hadn't been feeling well during the day and was withering quickly as the evening went on. After dinner, she decided to turn in for the evening and head back to the hotel room while Jill and I ventured to the Rio hotel for our Chippendale show. As soon as we got out of the cab at the Rio, Lisa called to say there was champagne and chocolate-covered strawberries in our room at the hotel. I told her to open the card. It was from Doug."

"From Doug?"

"Yes. I thought it was a little weird. I guess he was just trying to be a nice guy. I wished he hadn't done that. I didn't need him to remind me of what we had.

"But I decided that would be something Jill and I would enjoy when we returned to the room later that evening. There was no reason for it to go to waste!

"We picked up our tickets to the Chippendale show and then stepped outside so I could leave Doug a message to say thanks. I got his VM and just said that I appreciated he thought of me on my birthday and that I would be enjoying the champagne when I returned to the room that night. He never asked who I was traveling with, and still, I didn't know if he was aware it was Jill and Lisa. I guess he assumed it was a couple girlfriends since I don't think he would have sent chocolate-covered strawberries if he thought I was with another man.

"Jill and I found a bar to rest at, chat, and watch the Rio annual evening entertainment before our show. There were two women gambling at the tables directly behind us, and when one of them won eight hundred dollars, they popped over to our table to buy us each a drink. First time we were picked up by girls. Jill had a margarita, and I had a mudslide. We laughed because we both swore that one of the girls purposely brushed Jill's breast as she put down the drink on the table.

"On the way to the show across the casino floor, we stopped for an ass-kicking game of air hockey. We were still decked out in our beautiful and very sexy party dresses playing air hockey like two kids. Needless to say, Jill kicked my ass six to four. Once we finished, we were off to the show. Never saw so many men with rock-hard bodies who could dance. We were clearly on the older age side of the crowd, but we hooted and hollered like the younger girls and even got a butt groping from one of our cuter favorites as he walked by our row of chairs. Clearly, our cheap thrill for the evening. After forty, you enjoy the recognition when you can get it!

"Show was over about midnight, and we headed back to the Paris hotel. Once we returned to our room, we got into our PJs as quickly and quietly as possible, grabbed the champagne, two glasses, and the package of strawberries and then headed to the hall so that we didn't wake up Lisa. We headed to the center lobby of the eighteenth floor where we picked a quiet spot against the wall and uncorked the champagne.

"We sat there talking, laughing, taking pictures of ourselves with the champagne, and toasting Doug for sending it to me. After a few hours of enjoying our time together and the treats, we headed back to room 1893 and slipped the key through the lock, and the red light on the door kept going on. The door didn't unlock. We hadn't drunk the whole bottle of champagne, so I knew we were at the right room—so, we headed back down the hall and called security to send someone up and let us in. We were not going to walk through the lobby in our PJs. Not sure if I mentioned, but we didn't have any shoes on either. We decided not to bang on the door to try to wake Lisa because we didn't want to wake the folks in the rooms next door to us. Of course, we didn't have our cell phones with us either—so, there we stood outside our room, slightly buzzed and in our pajamas. It was hysterical!

"After ten minutes or so, security arrived and probed us on how we demagnetized our key. We had no idea. We just wanted to get to bed since we were leaving in the morning. After she drilled us about our IDs (which were locked in my room!), she finally agreed to let us in. Once we were in, I produced the ID and we were set free to sleep.

"Early the next morning, we woke up, packed our bags, and grabbed a bite to eat at the café in the hotel lobby before we jumped into a cab for the airport. We said good-bye to Jill as she left first to catch a Continental flight back to Florida. We then headed to Southwest and fought our way through huge lines for luggage check-in and security.

"Our flight was a little turbulent, but we arrived in Hartford safely and on time. As I dropped Lisa off, she thanked me for taking her on my birthday adventure and showing her that there is life after divorce and that it's OK to have fun and take charge of your life and enjoy things. I then headed home to see Courtney, Chloe, and Grandma.

The girls and Mom were playing computer games when I arrived and finished while I started to unpack and do some laundry. We only talked for a few minutes before Mom headed home. I was tired, and it was getting late. It was great to be home with my girls and getting ready to embark on a new year!"

Chapter 16

Dating Game

"It's a brand-new year. I'm forty. My life is good. I'm ready to move on and start taking care of myself along with taking care of the girls. My friends encouraged me join an online dating service. I didn't think I would go down this road, but then after a lot of encouraging, I decided to get back into the dating game."

"Really? What made you decide to go that route?"

"If you think about it, it was a safe way to meet men without having to hit bars. I have a lot to offer and none of my friends had gentlemen to set me up with, so I figured it was safe. I could screen in the privacy of my own home, and it would be fun. I didn't have time to go out and be trolling bars. Plus, my ex was an alcoholic, so why would I ever want to meet someone who was alone in a bar drinking?

"My online dating experience was like community dating. I got the insight from a few close girlfriends as we went through the screening of possible dates and had a lot of great laughs as we chipped away at the potentials—removed the short ones, the ones that don't make a lot of money, the ones that looked like pedophiles or ax-murderers, you know, all the normal screening mechanisms a few ladies would use. My married friends were living vicariously through my life. It was fun."

"Did you end up dating anyone through the service?"

"Yes, I actually went on a few dates with a professor from Yale. He was a little too artsy-fartsy for me and would wear his shirt unbuttoned with the chest hairs popping out the top—not a real turn on. Each time we were out, I had hoped to be able to engage in conversation, but I couldn't get past the chest hairs—like I was dating the America gigolo. I also spent a few months corresponding with a police officer in Massachusetts. Nice guy whose wife left him for another woman. He was the primary parent of his two boys. He had potential, but the distance would have been a problem. It was a good forty-five-minute drive between our homes. Quite frankly, neither of us would move. It was the Florida/Connecticut situation all over again, so we stopped it before it really got off the ground."

"Wait...Did you say his wife left him for another woman?"

"Yes. Imagine the baggage he'd be coming into our relationship with—probably a little too much to take on. There were some things that felt very much like high school all over again. Some guys rejected me (that hurt), and I had to reject some (still awkward because I was hurting them). I learned that at forty, no matter who I met, they'd have baggage. I have baggage. It's all about the levels of baggage. Some bring more than others into their next relationship. It's just part of who we are at this point in our lives.

"It was fun for the few months I did it. I purchased a three-month membership. By March, I had screened over a hundred guys, went out with about a dozen, and decided that although it was interesting, it really wasn't going to help me find my true love. I know it happens for some, but it wasn't working for me. It was too much work, and I was on the computer every day corresponding to folks via e-mail. It was very time-consuming and felt like a second job."

"How were the girls while you were going through the dating process?"

"They were OK. Having me going out on a date was no big deal. I'd already had periodic 'escapes' planned that I took. Every few months, I would check out for the day or a weekend to get some alone time.

"While I was doing the online dating, I had also started a friendship with a trainer at my gym. He was a forty-year-old ex-military man with very good looks and a wonderful personality. He'd flirt with me when I'd come in, and we'd talk about things we enjoyed in common, like the Caribbean, vacationing, and Jimmy Buffet. When I went in January, he was extra flirty, and when I left, he slipped me one of his business cards. On the back, he had written his personal e-mail address and a note that said 'E-mail me.' It was quite sexy to have a secret note passed."

"Did you?"

"Did I what?"

"E-mail him."

"Yes, I did."

"So you started dating?"

"Well, not exactly. Did I mention that he was living with a girl that he'd been dating for a few years?"

"So, what was he doing flirting with you?"

"Sarah, that's a good question that I asked myself a few times. I think there was a mutual attraction and he was at the beginning of the end of the relationship with his current girlfriend. I think he saw potential in us.

"OK, so we would e-mail each other with flirty little notes and we would meet up for coffee at a local bakery early on Sundays before my girls woke up. This went on for a few months, and it was fun. I never kissed him because he had a girlfriend and I thought that was crossing the line. But even without the physical connection, there was clearly some energy between us. One time, we laughed when we exited the restaurant door, as we both got a shock when we hugged."

"A little magnetic connection? Little bit of chemistry?"

"Yes. It was nice."

"So, what happened? Why didn't it work out?"

"It's complex when I try to explain. The abbreviated version is that we planned to meet for coffee on a Sunday and I was waiting for him there when he called my cell to say he was on his way. He called back fifteen minutes later to say that he'd just gotten a call from his live-in girlfriend that a pipe had burst and their condo was flooded and he had to go back home.

"That was the last time I agreed to see him outside of the gym."

"Why?"

"After I hung up the phone, I just sat there and thought, *Holy shit! I'm the other woman. I may not be physically involved with him, but he's having an emotional affair and he's just waiting for the perfect time to replace her with me. If he could so easily have an emotional connection with me and be living with her, what's to say he wouldn't do the same thing with me?* So, I went home and wrote him one hell of a well-crafted 'thanks but no thanks' e-mail. I was settling for less than I deserved, and I could see it so clearly. Even though I loved his emotionally wonderful e-mails that made me feel so good, I wasn't playing this role. I couldn't be that person for him. Maybe it would have worked for us under different circumstances but not at this time or this place. Sometimes it's just about the timing not being right. This was one of those times. I had to be number one in someone's life, not number two."

"Did you keep going to the gym?"

"Yes. Why switch when it's a good gym? I can tell you the first visit back after I sent that e-mail was a little bit awkward. He did brush his hand along my arm as I walked to a piece of equipment But, even with that said, I still go there. Things have become more normal as the years passed. I hope someday he will find a perfect match to share his life. He's a really nice guy.

"After my membership expired for the online dating service and I had to cut my gym friend loose, I decided dating wasn't for me. I would focus on my daughter's graduation, our upcoming trip, and getting her off to college. Finding a partner was turning into a job. I already had three jobs—raising my family, maintaining the house, and working full-time. I didn't need another job finding a man. I was good just by myself—at least for the time being."

"Are the girls seeing their father at all?"

"No, a year had gone by with no connection. I'd heard through my mother's relationship with him and his family that he was in recovery, but I couldn't let the girls get close to him again and have him fall apart and break their hearts. They never talked of him; it was like he didn't exist to them. I think that was their way to block out the pain. There was no contact."

"Sounds like you couldn't get involved either."

"It was a tough year, and there were times when I would be very angry and sad because I had to be mom and dad, providing encouragement and discipline, guiding Courtney through the process of selecting a college and praying that I was giving her the right advice. She and I did many college trips, and she was accepted to some excellent schools—Penn State, UConn, Pace, Michigan State, and Miami University, to name a few. We saw Miami while we were in Orlando in April, Penn State in the winter, and UConn in the spring. We weighed the pros, cons, and the academic scholarships, and she landed at UConn. It was rough going through this whole process myself, but she and I did it and we came out with a good decision. At UConn, I would still be able to pay for her four years even without any child support or alimony from her father based on the money I had saved over the years. I wanted her to have that bachelor's degree. I feel strongly that both of the girls should get their degrees. I only had an associate's degree at that time, and I always regretted that I didn't get my bachelor's degree when I was young."

"You know you can go back to school and get it?"

"Yes, I know. The problem is that at this time in my life, I didn't seem to be able to find the time or energy to go back to school. And although I knew I was facing the glass ceiling issues in the corporate world where my lack of a degree would hinder me, I was not sure that making more money was worth it to me at this time either. Through all this, I'd learned that money doesn't buy you happiness. It makes things a little easier, but you can accomplish what you need to get done whether or not you have money. I had to balance what my kids needed from me and what the corporate world could get from me. Do you know?"

"I have a spouse, so I'm able to get that balance. I can only imagine how difficult it is without someone to balance and debate discussions and decisions. I give you a lot of credit raising two daughters on your own."

"Thank you. I appreciate that. I did go back many years later and complete my degree. I'll tell you about that later on."

"Did your daughter graduate high school that summer?"

"Yes. There was a lot going on in May, June, and July of 2007. Let me see if I can get the order right and tell you all about it. Remember how my staff is trying to find the love of my life?"

"Yes."

"Well, in May, one of my employees thought I would find one of her husband's friends and business associates interesting and encouraged me to go out with him. Reluctantly, I agreed to take his e-mail and contact him. I sent him a quick note that night, and by the end of the weekend, I'd received an e-mail back that said that he had been mistaken for another of the guy's friends that I should have been connected with, so he forwarded my e-mail. Sorta weird, I thought. But, OK, whatever. If I heard from the other guy, I'd go out with him—and if not, oh well.

"On Monday, my employee was in my office first thing begging for forgiveness and apologizing profusely."

"For what?"

"Exactly. I had no idea what had happened. Turns out that the guy I e-mailed was the right guy, but when he found out I was forty, he said there was no way he could date me."

"How old was he?"

"Fifty. He would only date women in their thirties. What an ass, huh?"

"Seriously. A super jerk."

"Unfortunately, appeared to be somewhat common in guys. I wasn't mad. I just laughed and chalked it off as another jerk guy in this world. My opinion of men was slowly deteriorating.

"So, when my same employee came back a few weeks later and said she had the perfect guy for me, I was pretty hesitant to believe her. I think I actually laughed in her face."

"I'd be hesitant too. Her track record isn't so good. So, who was the guy?"

"He lived in her neighborhood and was divorced with two kids. He was a good dad with a good job, good-looking (she described him with short gray hair, blue eyes, six feet or so tall with glasses). Sounded too good to be true. I figured she was just trying to make up for her prior crappy setup. My staff, all women, were scouting out the universe for the perfect man for me. I love them for the fact that they cared about me enough to want to see me happy, but I was skeptical that there would be a good match out there, especially with what I'd seen."

"So, did you meet this guy?"

"I reluctantly handed over my personal e-mail address and told her that she could give it to him next time she saw him and if he e-mailed, I'd decide whether to correspond. He had a fifty-fifty chance I would actually respond to him. Let me just say, the odds were not in his favor based on the previous actions of the male gender."

Chapter 17

My Love, My Life

"Remember earlier when I mentioned that the last weekend I saw Doug was the same weekend that I met my husband? This was that weekend. I went away for one of my weekend escapes to Florida to hang out with Jill and Doug, and when I returned on May 21, I had an e-mail from Alex waiting.

"His e-mail was witty and sweet, and I thought, *All right, maybe he's not a jerk.* 'Tread lightly!' the little voice inside my head said. *Very lightly and then with thoughtful precision,* I responded.

"For the first week or so, we only communicated via e-mail. Every night, Alex would write me an e-mail, and every morning, before I went to work, I would read his note and e-mail him back.

"It was about a week into the relationship that we connected via phone. He was traveling for business, and we scheduled time to connect and talk one evening. It was a very nice conversation—comfortable and casual, nothing that we had to work on. It was very natural.

"So, on that sunny day in May, we both drove separately and met for lunch at the Grist Mill restaurant on the river in Farmington. We decided to take separate cars in the event that someone needed to 'escape' if it was horrible. It wasn't horrible. It was an amazing two-hour lunch where we just chatted and chatted. That was over seven years ago, and as they say, the rest is history."

"Let me get the cameraman's attention. Hey, Mike, can you pan out to the audience and focus on the gentleman with the blue shirt on and khakis in the seventh row on the right wing. Everyone, that's Alex. Hi, Alex."

"Hi, Sarah. Hello, my darling."

"Alex, I didn't expect you to be here! You were supposed to still be in Dallas on business. I can't believe you are here. I'm surprised that I didn't see you in the audience. I guess these lights are quite bright shining down. You'd think I would have spotted my husband! Oh, Alex, I'm so glad you're here, my sunshine. I love you, baby. Thanks for coming!"

"Alex, Sarah called out, come on up on stage and sit next to your wife.

"Can we grab another chair to put on stage, please?"

As Alex made his way up to the stage to sit next to me, he explained, "I grabbed the red-eye last night to make it here. Did you actually think I'd miss this day? It was a little tricky sneaking in here without you noticing me, but I think I did a good job. Sarah helped with the arrangements. Forty-five minutes into the show, and you didn't know I was here. I'd travel on trains, planes, or automobiles to be here with you. You know that."

Sarah turned back to Alex. "I'm glad we were able to get you here for Stephanie. Let's get back to how and when you fell in love. Is how Stephanie described your first meeting how you remember it?"

"Yes. We had a wonderful first date, and I had a very strong feeling that she was the perfect life partner for me the second week after we met. One night, while I was in New York on business, we talked for three hours. It was the most amazing conversation. Stephanie is the most amazing woman in the world. She is selfless, caring, loving, sweet, thoughtful, and an amazing mom."

"Stephanie, you're looking a little teary. You OK?"

"Yes. When Alex talks about me or about us, I get choked up. I can't help it. I'm a crier. I'm sure you already picked up on that throughout our conversation today. I love to listen to his voice with all the love and emotion as he talks about us."

"Stephanie, with Alex sitting next to you, all I can think is how your life has come full circle."

"I was just thinking the same thing. I think it often. How lucky I am. Hold on one minute so I can give him a hug and kiss...I'm good now."

"Man, you guys are so much in love you can just see it in the way you look at each other. It's beautiful!"

"Thanks. We do love each other."

"Even though there's so much love between you, it wasn't a smooth ride for you as you started your life together, was it?"

"It has been challenging. Alex is the love of my life. He is the most wonderful, romantic, sweet, kind, hardworking, and loving man I've ever met. We have been able to work through everything and anything, and although I might cry through a discussion, we would separate, take time to reflect independently, and then come back together and talk. I feel so blessed that he has become part of my life. I love him with all my heart. I thought the divorce would be the hardest part for the girls, but I think having a love enter my life was a significant adjustment for not only my girls but also for my whole family. It turned out to be a big issue."

"Have the girls adjusted?"

"Yes, I can say that everyone has finally adjusted and accepted. It wasn't easy. We've improved in dealing with the family challenges we've faced, and we expect obstacles will continue to arise that we will have to work through. I can't even begin to describe to you how much I thought through every single choice and decision that I made every moment starting when I found out Kevin had spent all our money until this day. I know every decision I make going forward will have that same level of scrutiny as well. I feel like I've put my responsibility as a mom, dad, caretaker, nurse, and counselor in alignment with every choice, but my family disagreed, and there have been multiple times over the past few years where I've been pretty beaten down because of my choices. It's taken a toll on my relationship with my parents and my girls.

"Someday, I hope that both girls and my family members understand all the choices I made and realize all that each choice was made with the girls' best interests in mind. I'm sorry for getting emotional. It's a difficult topic for me. I know realistically, this may never happen and I have to accept that."

Chapter 18

Graduation Incentives and Celebration

"OK, so you met Alex in May. In June, your daughter, Courtney, graduates high school. I understand that you did something really cool with Courtney and then later with Chloe to help incentivize them through high school."

"Yes, in retrospect, I think it was an excellent motivator for my daughters and a wonderful way to bond before sending them off with their wings to college. Before each girl started high school, so the summer between eighth and ninth grade, we signed a 'contract.'"

"A contract?"

"Yes, it started as a joke with Courtney and turned into a promise in writing for both girls. As any parent, I was worried about high school. As a single mom newly divorced, trying to balance all aspects of my life, I was worried sick. So, I told Courtney if she got through the four years with good grades, did not drink, didn't get pregnant, and got into good colleges, I would take her anywhere in the world for two weeks the summer between high school graduation and college as a reward for her success. Then she said, 'Put it in writing.' And we did. It was this handwritten 'contract' that we both signed and dated, and it hung on the side of our refrigerator for four years. It was brown and crinkly and dirty and nasty after four years, but it was right there every day reminding us of our promises."

"That's crazy!"

"I know. As adults, we want to have goals and rewards, and I thought it was important to create an incentive for my daughter, but it was a great incentive. Even Courtney said that she thought about it when she made choices during high school. I'll tell you about that trip in a minute. First, I'll tell you about graduation.

"I was so very proud of her when she graduated that June. She had five tassels hanging off her cap. She excelled in high school and graduated with many designations, including the National Honor Society, honors for science, honors for Spanish, honors for math, and CAPT scholar. I cried at graduation. She had made it, and I had done a good job teaching her right from wrong and helping her to become the amazing young woman she had become."

"Where was her father at this time?"

"Sitting a couple people down from me."

"What?"

"Yes, he began trying to reconnect through letters to the girls. Courtney didn't want anything to do with him. I didn't push. But I knew in my heart that although he had made bad choices and wasn't currently active in her life, he should be at her graduation. He was actively part of her life for fifteen years. He deserved it. I knew he was sober and employed since my mom kept in touch with him (which is a whole other story that we'll talk about in a few minutes), so I first asked Courtney if she would be OK if he was at her graduation. She said she didn't care, as long as she didn't have to talk to him. My interpretation of that was 'yes,' so I called him up and asked him if he wanted to go to her graduation. He did. In the end, it was Kevin, my mom, and me."

"Did Courtney talk to him?"

"No. And that was OK. She knew he cared enough to be there for her, and he was able to be part of a very momentous time in her life. He sat in the bleachers with us and quietly enjoyed the moment proudly. I had no regrets about including him—whether Courtney talked to him or not."

"That was very big of you to put your own emotions aside and focus on your daughter."

"So many people would rather fight with their exes. I believe that you need to tolerate the ex and focus on the kids—ensuring they come first. So, that graduation night, I sat next to my mom, who sat next to my ex, and I grinned and made it through a very proud mom moment!"

"So, where did you go for the two-week good-girl-in-high-school trip?"

"Africa."

"Really? That's where she chose?"

"Yes, she is adventurous. It came down to Egypt, Peru, Australia/ New Zealand, and Africa. It was exciting to plan the adventure even though I would be away from Chloe and my honey for eighteen days. That's a long time to be away, but I was really looking forward to this bonding opportunity with Courtney. We were scheduled to leave in July, which meant we had to get all of our shots to travel to Africa in May and June at the infectious disease center at the local hospital.

There was hepatitis, yellow fever, typhoid fever, meningitis, malaria, and tetanus, and of course, there was the patch for motion sickness.

"So, on a hot sunny July day, we drove to New York City and took a plane to London. We had an eight hour lay-over and ran around the city. We had a blast and then were 'stranded' overnight because of a broken plane. The next morning we flew to Kenya from there. It was an amazing adventure in Africa. We went to the Masai Mari on safari, hot-air-ballooned over the Serengeti at sunrise, visited a Masai village, and spent five days in Tanzania. We remember the first day we saw giraffes right in front of us and the cheetahs, elephants, lions, lionesses, zebras, and the wildebeest migration—hundreds of thousands of migrating wildebeests and we were right in the middle of it all! It was all so very amazing!"

"Alex, were you sad that she was leaving or worried about their destination?"

"Yes, of course. Eighteen days was a long time to be away, and I was very worried about two young ladies in Africa. I gave her something to keep me close to her heart."

"Really? What was it?"

"Alex gave me a wonderful photo book for me to take on my trip so that I wouldn't forget. I still carry it in my computer bag. Every trip I take, he's always with me. Here, take a look at it and you'll see how wonderful and thoughtful he is. The brown coach photo album about two inches by two inches opens into thirds. The first picture is of us in Elizabeth Park's rose garden in June the first month we met, a note in the center says, 'I hope you have a wonderful trip! Love, Alex,' and there's a picture of Alex in uniform (Boy Scout troop leader) on the right. Along with this, I carried a picture of Chloe in my backpack throughout Africa, and every time I felt a little bit lonely, I would look at those pictures and think of how wonderful it would be to come home and see Chloe and have Alex's arms wrapped around me."

"Was there anything scary about being that far away from home? In a third-world country?"

"We weren't scared when we were there except once in Tanzania, but then when we were home and we started to think about the vast wilderness we were in with no navigation/direction, we were a little more nervous about where we'd been."

"Did anything frightening happen when you were there?"

"Yes, there was one situation that freaked us out. While we were in Tanzania, the tour guide, who was a very large man, decided that he wanted me to be his American bride and made some inappropriate sexual advances that spooked Courtney and me."

"Give us an example. What did he do or say?"

"Courtney was keeping track of the animals, birds, and plants we saw, and one day, when we were driving to our next destination, he pulled out a very nice book that provided information on all the animal and plant species in Africa for her. What he said when he handed it to her was the part that upset us. His comment was, and I quote, 'When a male animal wants to mate with a female, they first make sure they treat the female's children properly.'"

"Eww."

"Yeah, that's what made us very uncomfortable. He was clearly referencing the book he was giving my daughter as a method of getting close to me. The day that he was coming on strong, we were out in the middle of the Serengeti sleeping in a tent that really had no protection. We were dirty, scared, and tired, and at that point, we just cried ourselves to sleep and asked the young man on vacation with his grandma in the tent next door (a hundred feet away) to keep an eye/ear out for us.

"During the night, you could hear the lions roar within a couple hundred feet of the tent. Probably what freaked me out the most, besides the giant tour guide, was the fact that there were poisonous snakes that could actually slither into the tents. We were advised to close the zippers extremely tight to ensure they didn't slither in.

"The morning that we were packing up and getting ready to head back to Kenya, he asked if I was married and stated that if I stayed in Africa, I could be his wife and would never have to work. He would take care of me, we would have babies, and I would have a wonderful life. I said, 'Thank you, but I have a boyfriend back in the States.' Then I walked away and jumped into one of the other safari jeeps, where Courtney was already sitting.

"There was such an amazing sense of relief when we actually crossed the border back to Kenya. I never said anything to Courtney, but I was scared for our lives, and I knew that in a continent like Africa, they still lived with laws not like the United States, and we could easily be abducted and no one would be able to find us/track us down."

"I didn't sleep for the last three days in Africa because I was so very frightened for us but couldn't show it. Our flight back to London was scheduled at eleven thirty one night, and we waited at the airport to depart, only to be informed that the flight would be delayed due to mechanical problems. It was around one in the morning when we finally departed. I actually started to cry as the plane's wheels left the ground.

"Why the tears?"

"Relief and joy. We had an amazing trip—even with the tour guide. Courtney and I survived another crazy experience in our life, and we became closer because of it. We pinky-promised we wouldn't tell our family about the harrowing experience."

"Did you tell the family when you returned?"

"Yes. Even with the pinky promise, it didn't take long to start spewing the story."

"What happened?"

"We had a family/friend gathering to share the pictures when we got home. My mother's best friend asked a simple question, 'Were you ever frightened?' Courtney and I just started giggling, and the whole story spilled out in minutes."

"Did you regret going on the trip?"

"No, not at all. As I mentioned before, it was a great way to recognize Courtney's high school accomplishments and send her off to her college adventure. It was also another confirmation to me that I was strong, I was independent, and I could take care of myself and my daughters. I was proud of traveling around the world, exploring an area I only saw in *National Geographic*, and helping my daughter to see that there are very different cultures and financial levels of people around the world. We are very fortunate to have all that we have."

"A few years later, when Chloe graduated high school, how did you feel on that special day? Did you go on a trip with her as well?"

"I was so very proud of her. She graduated with top honors and the designation of National Honor Society. She was very active in high school, being a great role model for the girls as the captain of the volleyball and tennis teams. She received the highest honor on graduation night when she was awarded the principal and faculty award. It was a very proud night."

"Was her dad there?"

"Yes, we were all there, including her dad's new wife. Over the years, we learned to put our differences aside when it came to big events for our daughter. We are socially accepting of the paths our lives took."

"Where did you go on her reward vacation during the summer between her high school graduation and first year of college?"

"Spain. We had a wonderful two-week trip. We started in Madrid and traveled along the southern coast, spent time in Morocco, and then traveled to Barcelona. It was a wonderful trip where we made amazing memories."

"Did you have any scary situations?"

"No, it was uneventful in a wonderful way—nothing scary and no one got hit on. Chloe and I had a wonderful time exploring and spending time at museums, parks, and historic places. She is a wonderful traveling companion, and I'd travel with either of the girls again, anytime."

"You must have been so relieved that the girls were successful in high school and they had turned out to be well-nurtured and very morally and emotionally developed."

"Yes, I am very proud. I know things could have worked out differently. I am thankful they turned out as they did, and I look forward to remaining an active part of their lives and their family's lives if they choose to marry and have children someday."

Chapter 19

The Angels that Watch over Us

"After that Africa trip, were you concerned that Courtney would be afraid to travel overseas?"

"Yes, I was. As I mentioned, Chloe and I traveled to Spain a few years later, and I've since traveled overseas to Prague, India, China, Singapore, and the United Kingdom for business but have no interest in going to another third-world country ever again on a vacation.

"Courtney, on the other hand, was planning to finish college with a bachelor's degree in international health care and poverty. She actually graduated with a bachelor's degree in biology. She has a heart of gold and continues to look for opportunities to support those who are less fortunate. She decided to sign up for a volunteer program to spend the month of January, her Christmas break, working in a pediatric children's hospital in Hanoi, Vietnam, and has since returned to Africa to climb Mount Kilimanjaro and work in an orphanage. Even Chloe has also gotten involved in overseas volunteering and has a trip planned to the Dominican Republic to teach English to children where English is a second language.

"Let me go back to Courtney's trip to Vietnam. I was hesitant to let her go, but at nineteen, she was an adult and independent. She wanted very much to go and help cancer-stricken kids. You would think that after the experience in Africa, she would be hesitant to try something again, but she was gung ho about taking this trip. So, in the middle of a snow-storm, Alex and I drove Courtney down to Newark, stayed overnight, and watched her get onto the plane the next morning. I cried on the way home. We stopped at a diner where we ate breakfast and I prayed silently that God would watch over her as she experienced this new adventure.

"It would be twenty-four hours later that she would actually land in Hanoi after a stopover in Detroit and then Japan. It was a very long twenty-four hours as I tried to go through my normal day's schedule and tried to stay focused on work as my daughter traveled alone across the world."

"Did she enjoy her trip?"

"I'd say no. Her four-week trip ended in five days. As soon as she landed in Vietnam, the nightmare started.

"She called when she landed and was through customs. It was about fourteen hours ahead of US time so around two in the morning in Vietnam and noon our time. She said she was fine so after sitting for hours and waiting for her to call and say that she was safe, Chloe and I packed up and headed to the gym. About an hour later, while I was sweating it out on the treadmill, my phone rang. I was panicked to see Courtney's name come across the caller ID. She said that no one picked her up and none of the phone numbers for the volunteer agency worked. A panic ran through my body from head to toe. My first reaction was this whole volunteer com-pany was a scam and she was a mail-order US bride!"

"You did not think that."

"Oh, yes, I did. Like lightning, we darted from the gym and drove home in record speed to track down the phone numbers for the agency to try to reach someone."

"Oh my God. You must have been freaking out. Did you reach someone?"

"After multiple attempts to various numbers, I finally reached someone in the Costa Rica office, who connected to Vietnam and sent a cab out to pick her up. So, picture this. She's in Vietnam. It's four in the morning, and she hasn't slept in over thirty-six hours. She is scared and abandoned, and no one speaks a word of English. I'm halfway across the world and can't help my crying daughter.

"I could tell she was really upset when she said that if one more Vietnamese person approached her to ask if she needed help, she was going to punch them. She was on the edge. Her cell phone was still working at this time, so she called back when the cab arrived and brought her to the hostel.

"That night, she was so frightened that she slept in the same room as the male volunteers. Turns out, she slept in the guys' room every night she was there."

"So, she's safe?"

"Yes, but we learned quickly that besides not getting picked up, she didn't have sheets or towels and had to sleep on a bunk with the blanket she took from the airplane. She was placed in a different location other than where she had filed as the location with the US Embassy, there was only breakfast, and the other meals the volunteers were on their own for, no safety orientation or program overview provided. Pretty much, she was a nineteen-year-old girl from the United States in a foreign country in an unsafe location and unsanitary conditions with no one who spoke English."

"Did she try to make it work? Was she able to get any volunteering done?"

"She tried for three days. She didn't spend any time at the hospital and left all of her gifts for the other volunteers to distribute for her. The doors at the house she stayed at were always unlocked, and there was no roof on the building so the chickens flew in and out. She actually did not have an opportunity to volunteer, to change a life. Well, maybe she changed her own a little but not that of the little children she had hoped for."

"Did you tell her to come home?"

"No. She wanted me to tell her what to do, but I knew that it was a no-win situation. If I told her to come home and she regretted not staying longer and trying, she would resent me. If I told her to stay and tough it out and something bad happened to her, I would never forgive myself. So, I told her she was the one who was living through the experience and she needed to follow her gut on whether to stay or leave."

"What'd she decide?"

"On the third night when she called, she told me she loved me and I needed to get her home safely."

"Was that strange?"

"Yes. She never tells me she loves me. Since she turned into a teenager, I can count the times she's said that on one hand. I knew she was emotionally spent and possibly in danger and I needed to work fast to get her home. So while choking back my tears, in the strongest voice I could muster, I told her I'd get her home. I said, 'Stay safe. I love you.'

"The whole day was spent finding flights to get her home. I lost all connections with her via phone, which I found out later was due to the fact her cell phone charger was moved with her luggage to another building. I finally got her flights out of the country through the US agents working through translators to connect to their Vietnamese counterparts. I spent twenty-four hours trying to confirm she was on the flights home through a translator in Costa Rica. It was by far the most stressful day of my life."

"Did you have the support of your family?"

"Well, not really. To be honest, if I'd told my family, I was afraid my mother would be so worried she would either have a heart attack or drive me to have one by calling every hour for a status. Alex, Chloe, and I were the only ones who knew. We avoided my family. If they asked how Courtney was, our standard answer was, 'She's fine, she's happy, and she's safe.' None of which were lies."

"She was happy?"

"Yes, she was coming home."

"She was safe?"

"She wasn't in imminent danger, so overall, I felt she was safe... maybe that one was a little stretch, but we needed it to keep everyone from worrying. I learned when she returned that she was the only American volunteer at the site during her stay.

"So, I finally got her new flights coming out of Hanoi to Japan and then to Detroit and finally Newark. I had to work through Northwest Airlines, who had to teletype information to Hanoi Airport since they were not on a computer system.

"Can I tell you one really cool part of this story? Not sure if you believe, but I believe we have guardian angels and there was an angel watching over her to bring her home safely."

"Yes, please, it sounds intriguing."

"I finally get the flights booked, and she has to pay the balance of the changed flight fee once she gets to Japan. In Japan, she goes up to the counter and the agent tells her she's twenty-five dollars short. She's stressed out to the max and hasn't slept in days. She goes to the ATM machine, and it doesn't give her any money. So, she calls me in tears. She's planning to miss her flight and wait until after midnight to be able to get money from the ATM and then she'll catch another flight. It's three in the afternoon in Japan. There's no way I was going to have her sleep in the airport overnight."

"So, what'd you tell her?"

"You're getting on that flight. Put your big girl panties on and approach someone in the airport and ask them for twenty-five dollars. She was like, 'No way!' I reminded her that it was just like the TV show *The Great Race*; they did it all the time. She could do it! In the meantime, I was working with the airlines to take my credit card and pay for the flight. Courtney headed to Starbucks and sat there to see if there was someone she could approach. She saw two men with four kids. She worked up all her courage, approached them, and explained the situation through her tears and promises that she would return the funds once she got back to the United States."

"Did they give her the money?"

"Yes. It turns out that one of the men grew up in Storrs, Connecticut, right next to the University of Connecticut where Courtney was going to college at the time. As if that was not coincidence enough, he was the principal of the American School in Japan and knew friends of ours who had relocated to Japan for a career opportunity. They gave her fifty dollars, and she returned to buy her ticket. Once she was back at the ticket counter, the steward advised her that it was two fifty and not twenty-five, as he had originally stated. Luckily, my credit card information was now in the computer, the ticket was purchased, and she was going to be on her way back to the United States.

"When I got home that night from Chloe's basketball game, I had a message from our bank stating that Courtney's debit card had been turned off due to potential fraud (too many countries in such a short time frame). It was a good thing she didn't wait until midnight after all. Nothing would have worked, and she would not have been able to get on the flight."

"As a mom, I can't imagine the fear you felt."

"As I mentioned, when she said she loved me through the tears in her voice, I knew I had to keep it together, get her home, and then break down.

"That morning, I headed to work and then called the airline to get confirmation that she was on her plane. The airline wasn't supposed to release the manifest. I understood that especially after Nine-Eleven, but I needed to know if she was on her way home. Finally, I reached a supervisor, and the gentleman confirmed she was on the flight. I finally exhaled. I think I had been holding it in for four days.

"During the whole ride from Connecticut to New Jersey to pick her up the next day, I prayed nothing would go wrong. I waited at the end of the concourse and made small talk with others also waiting. I had never felt such relief as I did when I heard the announcement that they were disembarking. When I saw her face, the tears just started to flow. I wrapped her in my arms and we walked silently to pick up her luggage.

"Courtney never said thank you for getting her home safely, but I know in my heart that she was just as relieved as I was to have her back on US soil. We drove home quietly with the sounds of the radio filling the empty space. She was exhausted both emotionally and physically. Just having her in the car next to me was comforting enough. The next day, we would talk."

"When did you tell your family?"

"That night, when Courtney was back in our kitchen, we called my mother and put Courtney on the phone. She was shocked to hear her voice but more shocked to hear the story."

"No good deed goes unpunished, huh?"

"Nope."

"How did she finance the trip? Did you pay for it?"

"Rich, I am not—and I've always taught the girls that they have to pay their way and earn things. Life does not hand out freebies. So Courtney wrote articles in the local papers to raise funds for her trip from both companies and individual donations. She also ran a few can and bottle drives in the neighborhood by leaving flyers on neighbors' mailboxes. Over two months, she was able to raise over two thousand dollars, which would fund her trip and allow her to bring toys and clothes to the children of Hanoi."

"She's quite committed to her goals, isn't she? Is she like you?"

"She was like I am at forty-three, but she was only eighteen. It's amazing to watch. As a mom, you want your children to grow up independent, but it's hard when they do because you feel you may not be needed any longer or valued for all you've done for them.

"I gave her roots to know where she came from, and I gave her wings to let her fly. Someday, I think she'll appreciate all that was done for her. Maybe someday."

"I am sure she already does."

Chapter 20

Define a Bad Parent

" The next year was very tough. I did not feel that I was valued by my family. It should have been the happiest year for me since I'd found someone I could love and who loved me, but it wasn't."

"What happened with your family? Why was it such a tough year?"

"When Alex and I met, we connected immediately and I knew after just a few dates that we were meant to be together. I knew that this would be a tough adjustment for the girls because they didn't have to really compete with anyone for my attention over the previous three years. It was just us girls, we got through everything together, and we managed just fine. It was a constant balance not to leave the girls alone too much but to be able to begin to see Alex on a regular basis. It became one night a week we would hang out at my house and then every Saturday night. I wanted to spend time with him. I wanted to spend time with my girls. A new relationship brings passion to spend time together, and that was challenging for the girls.

"Courtney had the tougher time with the relationship and would get Chloe all excited and upset whenever there was an opportunity to stir the pot. My mother was also very vocal, and she would never be able to communicate verbally, so, just like when I was a kid, when my mother had something to say, I'd get a letter."

"Letters?"

"Yes. I guess it was better than not communicating at all. The first letter came after I got back from Africa. I got home from the trip and hung out with the girls for a few hours, and then Alex came over in the evening for a few hours. I asked the girls if they minded, and they said they didn't mind. You'd think I was doing something horrible to them. My mother felt I was putting my emotions in front of the girls' needs. She told me that I never really loved Kevin like he should have been loved, and now that I had my first love, I was losing the focus on my priorities and my girls were suffering. I was so upset and wondered if she was kidding. I couldn't believe that she said that. It was such a cold and hurtful comment. I truly did love Kevin and stood by him for many years. This became the year of issues."

"What kind of issues?"

"Well, for example, Courtney would call my mother and tell her that I was always out (which I wasn't) and that I was neglecting them (which I was not). So, of course my mother would side with what she perceived as an issue without really understanding what was occurring or asking for my perspective. She had no concept that there are three sides to every story. I always believed you needed to hear them out—there's his, hers, and the truth. I don't believe that you should jump to conclusions when you don't know all sides of the story. Conclusion jumping was happening at every turn. It was exhausting."

"Did this create a lot of difficulty in your relationship with your mom?"

"Yes. I was always very close to my mother, so it was super hard for me to hear all the bad things she was saying about my parenting. And although she didn't use the exact phrase, she was very strongly implying that I was a bad mother, and that was a very difficult thing for me to accept. No matter how old you are, you look for your parents' approval. She had no idea how hard I worked to balance my choices and how much I talked to my girls about my choices and how they continued to tell me it was OK when I was going out with Alex or he was coming over. I would get someone to hang out with the girls, or I would let Courtney watch Chloe since she was a senior in high school. But it all got twisted."

"Where's their father through all this?"

"That was another issue that I was being hammered on as well. My mother had kept in touch with my ex all these years, and she wanted me to push my girls to reestablish their relationship with him. I *never* encouraged them *not* to have a relationship. I never said anything bad about him, and yet, I didn't feel it was my job to bandage up all their issues. All I could think was, *Man, how could that be my job too?* Didn't I already have enough to handle?"

"Did you eventually encourage them to reconnect?"

"I did end up having a few casual conversations with Chloe and Courtney regarding their father, but I never scheduled a get-together. When the girls were ready, they would accept his call when he rang the house.

"It was early summer that Kevin called and Chloe spoke to him again and began to reestablish a relationship. He was living with his girlfriend and her kids and was dry and sober. He had a job but still did not provide any financial support for the girls; it was all my responsibility and that was still tough on me. Even after having to deal with it on my own, it still made me angry and sad."

"So Chloe's reengaged with her father? Did that make your mother happy and more supportive?"

"On the contrary. Things got worse."

"Did things escalate with your mother?"

"Yes, unfortunately, there were a few big blowouts that fall, which would change our relationship. The one that really hurt happened on the day that I told the girls that their father was getting remarried. Of course, I had to tell them. I was the bearer of bad news. I sat Chloe down and talked to her to see if she was OK and then called Courtney, who of course said she didn't care about her father.

"That same night, I had a meeting at Alex's house since he was out of town to talk to the caterer about his surprise fiftieth birthday party in January. Chloe was home, and Courtney was away at UConn. I asked Chloe if it was OK for me to run out for a few hours, and she said it was OK."

"Did she seem OK?"

"Yes. She really did. She was watching TV when I left. I was gone about two hours and returned to the house to find Chloe, a box of Kleenex, and used snot balls across the living room floor, which I could see from the kitchen. I took one step into the sunken living room saying, 'What's the matter?' when I turned to the right and there was my mother sitting on the couch next to Chloe. I walked in and said, 'What's going on?'

"My mother said, with tears rolling down her face, 'This is an intervention.'"

"Was she serious?"

"Yes, she was dead serious."

"I looked at her and giggled a little because I couldn't believe what I was hearing. I thought it was a joke. An intervention for what? My first thought was that someone had been watching too much reality TV. You've got to be kidding me."

"Then my mother went off. It went like this: You are going to lose the girls like Kevin has. You are a poor mother, and you are neglecting the children." She continued with, 'If you don't change your behavior, the girls will move in with me and I will take care of them.'"

"I shook my head a few times thinking, *This can't be happening. Holy Crap, I was gone two hours. How could things have gone so terribly wrong?* I couldn't believe that she was actually threatening to take them away."

"What'd you do?"

"I took a seat on the fireplace hearth, looked straight at her across the room sitting on the brown leather couch, and calmly told her that she had overstepped her bounds, I wasn't neglecting the girls, and she needed to stay out of my life and my choices on how I was raising the girls. I'd had enough. Then, I took a breath and asked her to leave my house. She acted like I was physically, mentally, or emotionally abusing them. I hadn't done any of those things."

"Did she leave?"

"Yes. She angrily grabbed her coat, kissed Chloe good night on the forehead, turned, and walked out with a nice loud door slam behind her."

"You must've been thinking: *What the hell just happened?*"

"Yes. Clearly I was floored and needed to figure out what went wrong and how it happened. I started to piece together the night, and I determined that after I left the house, Courtney contacted Chloe via the computer and said things like, 'How does it feel to be abandoned by your father years ago and now that mom has a boyfriend, you're being abandoned again? It's like you don't have any parents left.'

"So, Courtney upset Chloe and then once Chloe was upset, Courtney called my mother to let her know that Chloe was left abandoned at home and she was hysterically upset."

"And?"

"My mom jumped in the car and went to fix what she perceived was broken. Later that night, I was able to take a look at the IM conversation between sisters. Want me to read a piece of it? It will help you to understand why I was so upset."

"Yes, please do."

"'Courtney (7:26:53 p.m.): Why do you have a problem with Dad getting married, but you don't have a problem with Mom never being around? He's not in our lives, but she is, and she's always out with Alex. Why are you having such a problem with Dad but not with her?'

"'Courtney (7:27:35 p.m.): You don't see her screwing up your life because she's never around?'

"'Chloe (7:29:03 p.m.): Yeah, I know what you're talking about, but ever since I was little, I was a lot closer to Dad than Mom, and it's just so hard for me to deal with him and Mom is trying her best to keep this family together.'

"'Courtney (7:32:36 p.m.): Like, I know you were closer to Dad, but we don't have him and now Mom's not even around.'

"'Courtney (7:32:45 p.m.): Do you ever feel like you don't have any parents?'

"'Chloe (7:33:30 p.m.): Yes.'

"'Courtney (7:33:13 p.m.): Are you crying?'

"Chloe (7:33:48 p.m.): Yup.'

"Courtney (7:40:42 p.m.): I'm gunna call Gma tonight.'"

"It's tough to read how the girls fed off each other that night. How'd that make you feel?"

"I felt horrible and very, very sad that they felt so strongly that I was making such bad choices and they didn't feel loved. Gosh, I love them so much. It was not comprehensible that they felt this way. I felt like shit that night, and every time I think about it or read it, I feel like a shitty mom.

"It was things like this that continued to occur, and of course, I was walking on eggshells and I felt horrible for how Alex must've felt to be on the rotten end of this."

"Did you stop seeing Alex?"

"No. I thought about it hard, but instead of cutting Alex out of my life, I cut back seeing him during the week, and then I talked with the girls and explained that I should be able to be happy again and love someone. It didn't mean that I loved them less. I had more than enough love to go around. Things might be a little different, and we'd all have to adjust. We needed to communicate and talk about what we were feeling."

"Did things get better?"

"They didn't get worse. Over the next year, things continued to be challenging. Courtney challenged everything I did and actually at one point said she couldn't stand living in our home because she didn't agree with the way I was raising Chloe. She felt Chloe would become a slut because of how she behaved and dressed. I couldn't believe this; it was the furthest thing from the truth. Chloe was a fun-loving four-teen-year-old high school student who was grabbing life by the horns. Didn't mean she wasn't a good kid or was going to make bad choices. It was very tough being judged and challenged on all decisions.

"Just like with my marriage, there came a day when I'd had enough with my mother and enough with my daughter and was not going to allow them to affect my life any longer. I needed them to jump on board and begin to accept the changes that were occurring."

"Or else?"

"Well, with my mom, I could separate her from my life. With my daughter, not so much. So I prayed there wasn't an 'or else' with Courtney."

"What were the breaking points?"

"For my mother, it was the spring of 2008 when she decided that she was going to call me as I drove to work one morning to let me know that she once again didn't agree with my method of child rearing and that she felt Alex should not participate in any family gathering so the kids were not upset. I lost it, totally lost it and began to scream at her and swear. I even dropped the F-bomb. And I told her I was done. She was never to give me advice again on a relationship unless I asked for it. If she could not accept my relationship with Alex and be supportive to help the kids adjust, then I was being forced to make a choice. I couldn't make everyone happy. I just couldn't. So, for the very first time in my life, I chose me—*me.* She could have a relationship with the girls but not one with me. I was having a breakdown. It was too much for me to handle. I didn't have control over what she thought of me, but I had control over how I dealt with it. Enough."

"Did it stop?"

"Yes. I stopped allowing her to upset me, and I stopped listening to what she had to say."

"OK, so you stopped listening, but did she stop giving her opinion?"

"It's stopped now, but for years, she would continue. I kept reminding myself that I could only control what I could control and that I had a choice on how to deal with her feedback. I respectfully listened but didn't hear."

"And what about your daughter?"

"For her, it was when Alex and I purchased the land for the new house."

"Oh, so you guys were planning to live together?"

"Yes, we were planning to build our dream home and bring our families together in a new home so we could start from scratch with a clean slate. At this time, I wasn't sure if Courtney would want to live with us, but that would be her choice.

"So, with Courtney, I was done having her give me a hard time about my life with Alex. I was always respectful of her relationships, and it was time she was respectful of mine. I knew it was hard on the girls, but they needed to realize that sometimes life just doesn't go the way you thought it might. Shit happens, and we all have choices on how to handle and adjust.

"Finally, when I pushed her to try to get to the bottom of her issues, she said she didn't want to be part of our new family, but she was afraid to say anything to me because she thought I'd stop paying her college.

"It was over a year since I'd been dating Alex. I agreed to pay for her four years of college, and I would do that. I would never take that away because she didn't want to live with us. Even if it broke my heart, I would respect her choice and not make her feel bad about it if she chose not to live with us as we planned to move into Alex's house or into our new home. She would have a room built, and she would be welcomed to it with open arms. If she decided not to come, then she would be twenty-one and old enough to start to live on her own, or I would ask my mother and father or my sister to allow her to stay there during her school breaks. It was time for her to also adjust to life changes and move on—one way or the other. She had choices, and it was time for her to make her choice and stop bitching about life's unexpected changes."

"How'd she take that?"

"She said she'd decide. She listened, and then we dropped it for the time being. It was still a few months before we sold the house and moved into Alex's house. I gave her the space she needed so that she could make her choice without feeling pressure to come with us if she didn't want to."

"When did she decide?"

"The night before we moved and had to move our last boxes."

"Nothing like going down to the wire, huh?"

"Yes. I had my parents and sister lined up if her decision was not to come with me. My heart was breaking, and I was praying I wouldn't lose her, that she would come with me. She never knew how devastated I was. This was her adult decision to make."

"And?"

"I asked her one last time. Where was she going to live?"

"And her answer?"

"'With you guys.'"

"Just like that?"

"Yup—a simple statement. No elaboration. No explanation. I didn't pry or ask. I was just very glad she did."

"So, your daughter finally takes a step in the right direction. Whew! That's one convert. How about Chloe?"

"Chloe was always more diplomatic. She tried to see the best in all circumstances. There were times when I know she was stressed out and didn't always want her friends over to our new house because she felt it wasn't her 'home.' That was tough for me because we used to always have friends over. I hoped that with time, she would adjust. Eventually, when we were in the new home we built, she had more friends over. This meant a lot to me because it seemed she was accepting."

"The girls are coming around. Why do you think your mother is having such a hard time?"

"I really don't know because she wouldn't communicate it. She never explained why she so badly wanted me not to be with Alex. She would just continue to make comments to redirect me back to my prior life, away from my current life.

"My opinion is that I think in some way she resented the fact that I divorced Kevin and she hoped that somehow there would be a miracle and we would get back together, that our family would be back together. Maybe she thought we were better off together as a dysfunctional family than a 'broken' family."

"Did you hear her say this?"

"Not directly, but I heard it through mutual friends and family who conveyed back to me that Mom was hoping Kevin and I would reconcile. When family members get divorced, everyone takes a side. I think it is human nature. However, in our divorce, whether she will ever admit it or not, by all her actions, I truly believe she took Kevin's side. She made a comment during the summer to my girls that she never left her husband when he was drinking (Papa) and that she stood by him through thick and thin. I think she felt I failed Kevin, walked away, didn't try hard enough.

"What I never understood and still don't get to this day is how she could be accepting of Kevin moving in with his girlfriend and supporting that relationship along with his remarriage, never showing me the support she gave to him. I always thought it was unfair that she never had problems with Kevin's choices, but she had huge problems with me having Alex in my life."

"Does that make you sad?"

"Of course. I really started to question my parenting skills. I was starting to think that I sucked as a parent and my kids were going to be screwed up messes and it would be my fault. My mother thought so, and my daughter thought so...maybe it was so.

"I always thought of myself as a good mom. I know the kids used to think of me as the 'boring one' and their dad as 'the fun one.' And you can hear in the IM chatter that they were closer to their dad."

"Do you think that's true?"

"That they viewed me as the boring one and liked their dad more? In their eyes, yes, I can see that. I was always worrying about work, money, the house, the bills, etc., and he didn't really have to worry, so he probably came across as more fun. In their eyes, they could have felt that he spent more time with them on weekends than I did when they were growing up since I was cooking, cleaning, grocery shopping, running errands, working to create a solid career, etc."

"Do you have regrets on how you raised them or handled the divorce?"

"Everyone has some regrets. I have some things I would change. Being an absent parent was not one of them. I was there for them. I have always been there for them—to guide and to love them. I will always be there for them. When your mother begins to articulate that you are not a good mom, that you're neglecting your kids, that you're selfish and not focused on the important things in life and you respect your mom as a good mother, you begin to think about whether what she says could be possibly true."

"How did you deal with all these thoughts and emotions?"

"I decided that I needed some external validation—either way. I needed someone to hear what was going on and tell me if I was screwing up my kids or doing things right, someone who could understand what was occurring in our lives and could give honest advice and perspective. If I was harming my kids, I would change. If I was not, then I would proceed and deal with the issues I was facing. My company has a wonderful employee assistance program so I decided to call it up and arrange for an appointment with a counselor."

"Alex, what'd you do throughout all this?"

"Listened and reinforced to Stephanie that she was a wonderful mom."

"Stephanie, did you meet with someone? What was their perspective?"

"Yes, I called a counselor and actually had four appointments with him. Cried through most of them, which is no surprise. I told him all about my history, myself, my kids, and the girls' relationships with their father, my relationship with Alex, and feedback from my mother. If I was being neglectful or doing something that would screw up my kids, I needed to know. If I was being selfish in wanting to have Alex in my life or moving too fast in a relationship, I needed to know."

"What did you learn?"

"That my mother was wrong. My counselor said that he could only wish that half of the single mothers would be as thoughtful and as supportive of their children and their children's needs as I had been/ currently was. I should not put my life on hold because the girls were having a tough time adjusting. He said that I needed to do what I was doing and give them time and eventually, at their own pace and on their own time, they would come around. I needed to move forward and follow my dreams, too. I had done good raising my girls and guiding them through the turbulent times of the divorce and divorce aftermath. I should continue to create a new life."

"And what about your mother?"

"He advised me not to listen to her. He agreed that she was having a hard time understanding why I would get divorced. He said it sounded like she had sided with my ex-husband, and quite frankly, she could never walk in my shoes and handle everything that I had to handle on my own.

"Because she hadn't been through my life, she would never see life from my vantage point. Her frame of reference was through a view that would never show the same reality of what I lived. He also said she could possibly be a little jealous that I had the courage to leave an unhealthy relationship and create a better life for my girls and she never had the courage to do that and wished she did. All speculation but at least it was confirmation that I was not doing bad things to my kids.

"He said I should be proud of all I'd accomplished, that my mom could have her opinion, and I didn't have to accept or listen to it and quite frankly, if things didn't improve, I might have to remove her from my life, not the lives of the girls, but my life until she could be supportive of my decisions and not undermine me."

"That sounds harsh—undermine you?"

"If you'd received multiple letters and phone calls telling you everything you were doing wrong in her eyes and one day walked into an 'intervention' because you were not a fit mother, *undermine* would be the word you would use to describe it too. She had lots of opportunities to reinforce to the girls that life changes and that I love them a ton and to talk to me about their feelings. But she didn't. It would have been so positive to have their grandmother reinforce, but she chose not to."

"That's a lot of tough relationship stuff going on, with your mom, your girls, and with Alex. It's been a while now since all this drama happened. How are things going now with your mom?"

"It's been a few years now. Things are OK. I'm not entertaining any conversations about my parenting, my choices, etc. If I want her opinion, I will ask. If I don't ask, don't give it. My closest girlfriends in the world would tell me if I was doing things that were not healthy for my girls.

"I used to share everything with my mom, and I miss the years we lost. We've gained a lot of our friendship back over the last few years and have gotten closer, but it's not like it used to be. I think we've both been changed with this experience and we're different adults, now. We accept and love each other for who we are."

"So you have all these challenges around you—bad vibes fighting against the love of your life. There were many attempts to push you back to return to your previous life, to challenge your choice to take this new road. However, you're still together. Let's talk about some things you've been through together and talk about your relationship.

"Shortly after you began dating, you received some bad news from an annual physical, didn't you? How did that affect your newfound relationship?"

"Yes, unfortunately I did get some bad news. During a routine pap smear, the results a few weeks later came back questionable. I went in for a cervical biopsy and was diagnosed with early-stage cervical cancer cells. That was hard to digest. All I kept thinking was, *Can someone just throw me a bone for a while, give me a few years of no drama?* But it wasn't the case. I needed to get through this."

"So, you go in for the normal yearly exam and get the call every woman dreads a few weeks later?"

"Correct."

"What'd you do?"

"Sat down, took a deep breath, and called Alex first and then followed up with calls to my parents and sister. I decided that my girls didn't need to know. They didn't need to worry that they would lose their mother to cancer when they already didn't have an active dad in their lives."

"Must've been difficult not to say anything to them."

"It wasn't too hard because I knew I was protecting them from scary stuff. But trust me when I say there were times when I wanted to scream at them and just say, 'Stop being so selfish and wrapped up in yourselves. You have no idea what others are going through! Don't be so judgmental!' I kept all those thoughts inside and never expressed them."

"The girls didn't know?"

"No, I had the biopsy done when they were in school and just told them I had my period and that was why I was lying on the couch relaxing for a few days."

After the biopsy returned the positive test results, I was scheduled into the office for the procedure to remove all the precancerous cells and burn all the cells around the bad cancer patch to ensure they were all gone. Both procedures caused me some significant discomfort. I was crampy and bleeding for a few days after each procedure, but other than that, it was done. Waiting for the results to ensure the bad cells were burned was a horrible time. Waiting and waiting. Days dragged by. Finally, about a week later, I received the call from the doctor."

"Good news?"

"Yes, the test results came back negative."

"What did that mean?"

"All the bad cells were removed. I would now start pap smears every six months, and we'd see what that brought. Waiting for results after each test was very difficult."

"How'd it go?"

"I had the first pap smear after six months, and it came back negative. I was feeling much better. I've been clear for four years now and just moved onto an annual pap test again. What a relief!"

"That must've been tough on both of you. Alex, how did it affect you?"

"All I could think is that I finally met the woman of my dreams, the love of my life, and something bad happens. I told God he couldn't take her. It just wasn't going to happen. I was up for a fight."

Final Chapter

My Happily Ever After

"With everything you've been through and all the adjustments in your life, what worries you now?"

"There will always be things I worry about. I don't think that will ever change. I still worry about the effect of the divorce on my girls. I will always worry that I'm not being the best mom for them, that they will resent something I have done or something I haven't even done yet, that I'm not giving them everything they need. I will worry about that for the rest of my life. I worry about money and about my financial independence. I don't think I will ever gain that complete sense of security again. I will always worry that someone else will burn me like Kevin did. I worry that the drama of combining the families will create a rift between Alex and me that we will be unable to communicate through and deal with. Lastly, I worry that just as Alex and I settle into our wonderful life, something bad will happen and it will all blow apart. After so many years of disappointment, I still pinch myself to ensure I'm not just dreaming and things are really as good and as wonderful as they are."

"Tell me about your plans as a couple. You are clearly very much in love; we can all see that when we look at you. Do I see an engagement ring and a wedding band on your finger?"

"I mentioned that we had sold our home and moved to Alex's home with his family for about a year while we built our dream home. We built a beautiful home located in western Connecticut on about two and a quarter acres of beautiful maple, birch, oak, and pine trees. Protected land surrounds our lot, which will ensure no one will build behind us. Just the cow, chicken, and turkey down the street and the deer and bear that roam behind and around our home will be our neighbors. We're a few blocks off a main street in a development with about ten homes in it. We're at the end of the cul-de-sac with one neighbor a few hundred feet to the west and no one to the east. It's a craftsman/bungalow-style home covered in cedar natural-stained shakes, batten board on the walls under the porch topped with a deep green metal roof with white six-inch trim surrounding the prairie-style casement windows. And the best part is that we have a matching shed. We actually call it a 'carriage house' instead of a shed. It sounds so much nicer. Plus, it's sixteen by twenty-two, so bigger than a shed. It is really an extra garage that keeps all of our gardening supplies. The front overhead allows for a great location to do my gardening with the custom-crafted potting shed my darling husband built for me. It has one window to host my flower box filled with petunias in the summer, pumpkins and gourds in the fall, and pinecones and red berries with greens in the winter. Nothing like a flower box to welcome friends to our home.

"It took us about a year to design and another year to build. What an amazing experience for us to be the general contractors and make this happen. When you look at it, it's wonderful because we have the pleasure of knowing we created that home. Alex and I did. That's enough baby for us. It's the only thing we'll be creating."

"Are you in the new home?"

"Yes, we moved in about three years ago. Every time I drive down the street, I still get goose bumps. It makes us proud to see that we accomplished and built this beautiful home together to start a wonderful life."

"So tell us about the engagement. Women love to hear the romantic story."

"We've always planned to get married in the house or on the property. Whenever we do something at the property, we always stand 'at the front door' and admire the view from the front door. When we were laying out the location of the house, we mapped out where the front door would be and imagined our friends and neighbors driving up with us sitting on the white rockers that adorn our front porch and watching absolutely nothing but the wildlife. It was 'at the front door' the day after Thanksgiving that Alex proposed. We always joked that maybe we'd say our vows on those front door steps some day!"

"We all love the story of a marriage proposal. Would you tell us how Alex proposed?"

"Sure. It was a Friday, and we had gone out for the day to mark and cut down our live Christmas tree, which was at a farm not more than two miles from the location of our new home. It was a sunny, cold windy November day. The air was filled with a winter chill and the hint of snow on the brink of falling. We walked throughout the tree farm and finally tagged the tree we wanted. As we headed back to pay and pick up our free candy canes, Alex asked if it would be OK if we stopped at the property to measure out the location of the front door against the line of the wetlands. Although I was freezing, I agreed and we headed to the house. I held one end of the hundred-foot tape measure, and Alex held the other. We measured a few of the points to the house, and then Alex walked back toward me as I stood there shaking in the cold under what turned into a cloudy/overcast sky. I turned to ask Alex if we were ready to head home and grab a coffee. He walked up behind me and said, 'I just have to do one more thing before we leave.' I said, 'OK,' and turned around to see him drop to one knee and pull a ring box out of his pocket. He said, 'Stephanie, I love you with all my heart, will you marry me?'"

"And you said?"

"'Yes, of course!' Then he opened the box and slipped the ring on my finger, and we kissed as the tears of joy and happiness rolled down my cheeks."

"At the front door?"

"Yes; well, the future location of the front door. With snowflakes falling gently from the sky, my toes frozen, and my heart racing we left the property and headed to pick up that coffee to warm up our hands and our toes. Our hearts were already filled with love and warmth."

"How long were you engaged before getting married?"

"Almost three years. We've known each other almost seven years now."

"So what held you back from getting married quicker?"

"First priority was to determine if we could successfully blend our families. To be honest, it's been really tough for each of us and our relationship. I wasn't ready for it. I hadn't prepared myself for all the difficulties we would face. Remember, according to the fairy tales, we all fall in love and live happily ever after. I figured that Alex and I could take anything on, that things would fall into place, our kids would get together, everyone would get along, and life would be bluebirds and rainbows—one happy family."

"I take it it's not been a smooth blending of families?"

"We have had our share of rocky moments."

"A lot?"

"Enough. More than either of us would have liked."

"You shared a lot a lot about the history you brought to the new relationship. What about Alex, did he have a lot of history?"

"Yes. Anyone at our ages and taking on a second relationship brings a lot of baggage with them. I think the way I would summarize his baggage would be that Alex was married for around fifteen years to a woman who wasn't his equal. He was the primary breadwinner, did the majority the work around the house and had to find time to spend time with his children while traveling a lot for his profession. He was ambitious and she was lazy. That's a mix that doesn't work long term. Over the years, resentment built up and the relationship began to deteriorate until one day, there was no more to work on. Alex became focused on himself and his kids and he stayed in the marriage miserable for far too many years. He turned to enjoying wine as his escape in the evenings to block out all the pressures of work and an unhappy home life. Luckily, one day he woke up and began to move on with his life – leaving his wife. Once he made that break, he found his freedom and happiness and has never taken a drink since. One of the challenges he faced through the years was 'leaving' his kids. Although they had equal parenting time, he always felt *absent-father* guilt."

"So besides the baggage you each brought to the relationship, what have the challenges been?"

"I'd sum it up in two: One, we've raised our kids differently, so our disciplining and rewarding structure is not the same. Two, the kids are very different in their drive and ambition so they didn't always see eye to eye, which goes back to number one. We're making it work, which is the good news. There are so many dynamics that go into a blended family. There are so many challenges that no one talks about or prepares you for when you embark on a new relationship. Even now, after being married for so many years, we all don't get along. Most of us do, but not everyone. Once I figure it all out, I may write a book… There are probably a host of opportunities for others to learn from my experience. I've had a few more trips to my favorite counselor over the last three years. It's always helpful to talk to someone about the family dynamics and how I feel about the family interactions and my hesitation to marry."

"Did you gain any insight?"

"Yes. I received confirmation that my feelings are normal under the circumstances and that I would be able to tell when I was comfortable that our relationship would sustain the challenges of the family dynamics. I also learned that I can't let the kids rule our decisions.

"There's one thing I was always sure about—although I delayed the wedding plans, I was never going anywhere. I was committed to building the life I always dreamed of with Alex. The legal part of the union just took a while."

"If you weren't leaving, why not marry?"

"My logic may sound stupid, but by not being married, I could separate myself from the dynamics I didn't agree with or I didn't want to be part of. I didn't have to do family vacations, and I didn't have to explain why my kids got something that maybe his kids did not. Also, we kept all our finances separate so we were responsible for our own bills and savings. I felt it was better this way. I hate to say this, but I could run away when I needed to disengage from any of the drama for a day or a weekend and I never felt guilty."

"Alex, you agree with Stephanie on the family dynamics?"

Alex said, "Yes and no. I think it's more challenging for women to adjust. For the guys, they can go with the flow more. I think that the ex-wife situation I have to deal with is different than Stephanie's ex-husband situation so it adds a different level of complexity. With Kevin not involved in the parenting aspect of her girls' lives, she had more control over how the girls were raised. Him not being present in their formative years was also a detriment to them emotionally. My ex-wife was around; she just wasn't an amazing role-model mother, but my kids did spend time with her.

"Her girls had their mom to themselves for a few years, so sharing her was not easy when I came into their lives. I think seeing how hurt she was by the divorce; they didn't want to see her hurt ever again. I was a risk. I could have hurt her. My kids had a different perspective. My son was very encouraging of the relationship and my daughter; she was a teenager who was looking for the parent of least resistance so I think she was indifferent.

"There were a lot of family traditions Stephanie had, and with divorce, everything changed. Then, here I come, and things start to change again. I understood what they were going through, and I would have waited a lifetime until Stephanie was ready to be my wife. Luckily, I only had to wait three years."

"Alex, would you say you are happily married?"

"Absolutely. I love the life we share. I love spending time with her doing mundane tasks like cooking or grocery shopping. I love drinking coffee in our white rocking chairs on the front porch after dinner and talking about our day. I love taking a road trip in the western hills of Connecticut or doing projects around our home. She is my calming element. No matter how crazy things get at work or with the family, I always know our home is a place full of love, respect, and joy. I am proud to introduce her as my wife. There is no better feeling in this world than to know you have selected a partner who makes you proud.

The adversity she faced, the girls that she raised, the career that she managed, and now the foundation she has founded speaks volumes about who she is. She always sees the glass half full, and I am confident through her work in the foundation, she will be changing the lives of many women. I am sure she will tell you more about her foundation in a few minutes."

"Stephanie, any thoughts?" asked Sarah.

"You can see why I love him so—"

Sarah saw that the producer was waving her down and turned to the audience. "We need to take a five-minute commercial break. We'll be right back to close out our interview."

She turned back to us. "Stephanie and Alex, I can't thank you enough for coming today and sharing your story. We have about ten minutes left before we wrap up. After we conclude, please stay for a guest reception. The production team and I would love to have lunch with you before you head back home."

"Thank you, Stephanie responded, we'd love to stay for lunch."

As the lights came back to full strength, Sarah turned to the audience. "We're back and will touch base on how the family has adjusted now that Stephanie and Alex are married, catch up on Stephanie's latest personal triumphs, learn more about the foundation and wrap up with some closing thoughts." Sarah turned her attention back to me, "And how's Courtney now? Is she still stirring the pot with her sister?"

"No. The kid who created the most turmoil is the one who brought my family together with Alex's family."

"Really? How?"

"She was twenty, a junior in college, and getting ready to return to Africa to climb Mount Kilimanjaro and volunteer at an orphanage. Before she left, she asked if we could get the whole family together for a good-bye dinner. My reaction was to have just my immediate family go out to dinner and avoid the drama that would come with trying to convince my parents to come to Alex's house. I told Courtney we'd schedule dinner at a restaurant and she said, 'No.'"

"That's great."

"Yes. She wanted everyone over to 'our house,' so that was what we did. Chinese food and the whole family over."

"So, it was the kid least likely to accept life's changes who matured, accepted the changes, and brought the families together?"

"I know—ironic. Since then, we've had a few family gatherings, and the following fall we all had Thanksgiving at our new home. We may not always be one big happy family, but we're slowly becoming one accepting family."

"How are things with your ex-husband now that so many years have passed? How is he doing with the girls?"

"I am very happy to say that he is doing really well. He's remarried and seems to be happy, sober, and drug-free. He has a relationship with Chloe, but Courtney isn't interested in reconnecting with her father. I am not sure if she will, but if she chooses to, it will be on her own schedule. I'm OK with that. She may choose to forgive as I have, or she may never be able to. My counselor told me many years ago that will be her choice and no one else's."

"Is it also true that you went back to school after all these years to complete your bachelor's degree?"

"Yes. I started in January 2011 to pursue my bachelor's degree at night through an accelerated program at a local college. One of my former coworkers and good friends signed up to pursue her degree as well. I graduated cum laude with a business administration degree in May of 2013. It may have taken me twenty years to get it done, but I'm glad I did. It was a personal accomplishment, and it felt great."

"So, in one year, you've built and moved into a new house, started a new job, and went back to school. On top of all these actions, you were also focused on raising two amazing daughters?"

"Yes. When you put it like that, I guess that year was quite the accomplishment for me."

"Anything else in your future plan that is life-changing?"

"I don't see anything upcoming that I would consider life-changing. The kids are settling into their own adult lives. Courtney is married to a very nice young man, teaching high school math and living down South, and Chloe is finishing up her college degree in New England, working her summers as an event-planning manager and running many nonprofit activities throughout the school year while playing tennis and maintaining A's and B's. She has been dating a very nice young man for the last five years, and I'm sure there will be some wedding bells in the future for them. Alex's son, Brett, and his daughter, Melissa, are both in New England working. He continues to stay in touch with both of them on what's occurring in their lives as they transition to young adults and develop their own independent lives.

We're hoping things stay quiet and we can enjoy our home and family on weekends and spend time during the week working on the foundation's mission."

"I hope your daughters know how fortunate they are to have you as such an amazing role model. I'm sure they are very proud of you."

"Thanks. I think they are. When I started my new job, I received a card and gift from Chloe saying how proud my daughter was. Although they don't express their approval that often, I cherish the moments they do. I know that whatever I am doing or saying they are watching me. I hope that the day that I leave this world, both of the girls can stand in front of our family and friends and say, 'Stephanie was an amazing mom and an amazing person.'"

"Our time is almost up. I can't thank you enough, Stephanie, for coming here today and sharing your story with us and, Alex, for taking the red-eye from Dallas to be here to surprise Stephanie. Before we wrap up, you need to tell us all one thing: did you ever get to Paris?"

I could feel the smile begin on the left and spread across my face until my eyes were twinkling. I looked lovingly at Alex and slowly reached for his hand to intertwine our fingers.

"Yes, we did. March of 2011, Alex and I spent a glorious week in France. Paris is a magical city and truly the most romantic vacation we have ever been on. Although I may not have made it for my fortieth birthday, I made it a few years later with the love of my life. We enjoyed all the romance and excitement that Paris could offer."

"Hugging and kissing all over town?"

"Yes, of course. It is the city of lights and the city of love. When we landed, we headed to the hotel and dropped off our bags and then walked down a street to begin to explore the city. Unknowingly, the direction we took headed us straight to the Eiffel Tower. As we turned a left at the end of the street, I stopped dead and there, standing right in front of me, was the tower in all its beautiful glory. I was speechless and overwhelmed by emotion. It was spectacular. I was standing in Paris! Standing there meant so much to me. I had survived all the challenges, I had found my strength, and I'd found my happiness. I found me. I had arrived. There was nothing this girl couldn't do. Even now, in my mind's eye and in my heart, I can recall how that moment felt. I will cherish it for the rest of my life.

"About three days into the trip, as we sipped on our coffee and ate chocolates outside our favorite café, with the view of the Seine River and the tower lit up with its sparking white lights, Alex asked me if Paris was all I'd imagined and had dreamed it would be."

"How did you respond?"

"I turned to him, cradled his face in my hands, brought his lips to mine, and kissed him. When our lips parted, I looked into his eyes and summed it up in one word, '*More.*'

"In September of that year, we held the wedding we'd dreamed of. We like to describe it as a celebration of friends and family, where a wedding broke out. We've both been through so much in our lives and in our own divorces that it is nothing short of a miracle that we found each other. Building our dream home and doing a lot of the work together is such an example of our relationship and how we approach everything.

"We exchanged our vows and committed our lives together in front of seventy of our closest family members and friends under a white tent on the front lawn of our new home. It was a wonderful day."

"We are glad to hear that you finally tied the knot.

"Alex mentioned the foundation . . . . tell us a little more about what the focus is."

"I'm excited about the foundation. For me, it's all about paying it forward. The company is called Sunrise Foundation For Women, Inc. Our mission is to raise funds that can be disbursed to women based on their individual needs to help them financially to leave a bad relationship and begin a new life. The website is *www. Sunrisefoundationforwomen.com.*

"I hope folks will take a few minutes out of their busy days and think about women they know who may be in an unhealthy relationship but are unsure how to get out. Direct them to the website for assistance. We can provide the tools and the support to those who are bound by fear. Change can be paralyzing, but taking the first step is all it takes to move forward. One step turns into two, and from there, it's a jog and a run. The first step is the hardest. They can get out and have a better life. I am an example, and I want to be the change to inspire others."

"I am guessing you selected the company's name based on how much the sunrise meant to you in your darkest days. Am I correct?"

Stephanie started to smile as she quietly responded, "Yes."

"Let me ask you one more time. Is there anything that you would change if you had the opportunity to do it all over again?"

"No. Honestly, I wouldn't change a thing. I am who I am because of everything I experienced and how I chose to handle each situation. I would not be here in front of you and the studio audience without having been through it all. I said it before and I truly believe that every-thing happens for a reason."

"We have two minutes. Leave us with your summarized thoughts on what you've learned and what we can learn from you."

"I would be happy to, Sarah. Before I share, I just want to remind everyone that making a significant life change is not easy, and as you can see from my experience, there are many people who will try to make you change your mind. You will get advice from people who think they have your best interest in mind when they haven't walked a step in your shoes. If you have children, they will try their hardest to put life back together where they were most comfortable, with their mom and dad together.

"Here are my top five takeaways for the audience: One, control your own destiny. You have choices. Make them, no matter how scary. Two, tackle anything by breaking it down into manageable tasks. When you look at the whole, it can be overwhelming and paralyzing. Lay life's challenges out like a project plan or a to-do list, and check things off one at a time. Always remember, you can eat an elephant…one bite at a time. Three, own your feelings. No one has the power to make you feel bad or guilty about your choices, and no one has the power to make you do anything you don't want to do. You cannot change what someone does or how someone else feels. The only thing you can control is how *you react*. Four, recognize that each day is a gift. It is not something that should be taken for granted, and it should be lived. Never let the opportunity pass to tell someone how much you love them. Surround yourselves with the friends who will be there in good times and bad. Shed all the negative people. Forgive; it releases you. And five, mean what you say. Words are biting and can never be taken back. Once they leave your mouth, you have affected someone else—either positively or negatively. Choose positive words. Build someone up. Don't knock them down. Before you speak, ask yourself these three questions: Is it true? Is it necessary? Is it kind?

"My husband always says words are like toothpaste; once it's out of the tube, you can't put it back in. We have no idea what goes on behind closed doors, so be kind to others. They may be traveling a harder road than you. When your life is blessed, bless others. The one act of kindness you grant may change someone's life. We are placed into the lives of others to bring out the best in them and help them. In the process, we become a better person.

"My life is a spectacular unfinished story, which will be full of exciting twists and turns, loves and sorrows. I welcome each sunrise with open arms. I am blessed with a loving family and amazing friends. My parents once told me when I was a young lady that love could never be found in materialistic things. Love is found in the heart. Granted, it took me quite a while, but I now understand exactly what they meant all those years ago.

"Thank you for the opportunity to share my story. I hope I've helped someone think differently about their life and their choices today. Sometimes all we need is one person to help us see the forest through the trees and to believe in us when we don't believe in ourselves. I hope that one person will think about their choices a little differently than they would have before the start of this show."

"Thank you so very much for coming and for having the courage to share your life experience. Behind us on the screen is one of your favorite quotes that I wanted to share with the audience as we close out the show. *'Don't listen to people who tell you what to do. Listen, instead, to the people who encourage you to do what you know in your heart is right.'*

"I want thank the audience for their engagement in our discussion. I hope you walk away with something positive from the last hour we spent together. I'm Sarah Swanson signing off of **The Morning Show**. We'll be back tomorrow with Michael Allen, who will share with us his recent photographic memoires as he took a year off of work and trekked across the Himalayas. The faces of the people he encountered each have a unique story that he will share with us. Enjoy the rest of your day."

Acknowledgments

To my daughters, words alone cannot describe how unbelievably proud I am of my beautiful, smart, and loving daughters. Be strong, and take your life to where all of your dreams will be fulfilled. Only you can stop yourself from reaching your highest achievements. Strive for the stars because you have the power to succeed in whatever you choose to do. Wherever life takes you, you will always be close to my heart, and you know where home is. I am always just a phone call away.

Mom and Dad, thank you for loving each other and bringing me into this world. Your support and love over the years has been inspirational as I found my way. You continue to be wonderful parents and grandparents to the girls. Thank you.

God blessed me with the best sister I could ask for. Your influence in the girls' lives provided strength and structure during the difficult years when they needed it.

Wine Girls and Work Girls, you've been there through good and bad. You've seen me at my best and my worst. Every woman needs a friend who will tell her like it is, provide the shoulder to cry on, pour the wine, and hand over the tissues. I am very fortunate to have many.

Lastly, my love, thank you for loving me for who I am and being my biggest supporter and partner in this crazy life. We weathered our own storms to find the calm in each other's arms. I look forward to all the adventures we have yet to experience. Together, we will write the best never-ending love story.

"Anyone can give up. It's the easiest thing in the world to do. But to hold it together when everyone else would understand if you fell apart, that's true strength."
—Anonymous

Thank you
for Supporting
our foundation

Love

Thursa

About the Author

The photographer is:
Erin Wood Photography, Southington, CT

Theresa Valentine is a global payroll director and a seasoned corporate professional with more than twenty-five years of experience in human resources and payroll management. She graduated from Albertus Magnus College in 2013 with a bachelor's degree in business management and now lives in New Hartford, Connecticut, with her husband, Joe, and family. She is proud mother to two grown daughters.

Now that her children are adults and her career is settled, she is sharing her personal story, giving back, and helping others. Drawing on her business management and leadership skills, as well as her personal insight into the topic, she founded Sunrise Foundation For

Women Inc., a nonprofit organization committed to helping women in destructive relationships find the strength, support, and resources they need to take the step toward a healthier life.

For more information, please visit sunrisefoundationforwomen. com.

Made in the USA
Charleston, SC
01 January 2015